"That fella you're writing. Is he anyone special?"

Amity blinked. "I'm surprised you recalled that."

"I pay more attention than you think I do."

She paused a moment before answering. "I've only gotten one letter so far. But it was quite sweet. He's, um, interested."

Curiosity prodded at Ethan. "You planning to write back?"

She laughed. "*Ja*. I think I will." Crossing her fingers, she comically bit her lower lip. Her nose scrunched in the cutest way. "Who knows? This might be the one."

As they conversed, Ethan's fingers nervously intertwined with the edge of his suspenders. He tried to suppress the pounding of his heart, but it was futile. The realization dawned on him like the first light of a new day. He was jealous another fellow had her interest.

The newfound emotion was exhilarating. And terrifying. Her hopes reflected his own yearnings.

The ice chilling his emotions had, at long last, begun to thaw.

He felt a presence, as if *Gott* was guiding him gently forward...encouraging him to embrace life once more.

Pamela Desmond Wright grew up in a small, dusty Texas town. Like the Amish, Pamela is a fan of the simple life. Her childhood includes memories of the olden days: old-fashioned oil lamps, cooking over an authentic wood-burning stove and making popcorn over a crackling fire at her grandparents' cabin. The authentic log cabin Pamela grew up playing in was donated to the Muleshoe Heritage Center in Muleshoe, Texas, where it is on public display.

Books by Pamela Desmond Wright

Love Inspired

The Cowboy's Amish Haven
Finding Her Amish Home
The Amish Bachelor's Bride
Bonding over the Amish Baby
Her Surprise Amish Match

Visit the Author Profile page at LoveInspired.com.

Her Surprise
Amish Match

PAMELA DESMOND WRIGHT

LOVE INSPIRED
INSPIRATIONAL ROMANCE

LOVE INSPIRED®
INSPIRATIONAL ROMANCE

Recycling programs for this product may not exist in your area.

ISBN-13: 978-1-335-93671-4

Her Surprise Amish Match

Love Inspired
22 Adelaide St. West, 41st Floor
Toronto, Ontario M5H 4E3, Canada
www.LoveInspired.com

Printed in U.S.A.

But if we hope for that we see not,
then do we with patience wait for it.
—*Romans* 8:25

For Claire Matturro

My dear friend, mentor and go-to beta reader.

Much praise also goes to my editor, Melissa Endlich, and my agent, Tamela Hancock Murray. Both ladies are super-savvy and smart, and keep me on track when doubt creeps in. I couldn't write these books without their guidance, wisdom and encouragement. I'm happy they have come along for the adventure.

Bless you all!

Chapter One

Ethan Zehr watched the hustle of activity outside the window of his *kaffeeshop*. Workers with boxes were going in and out of the retail space across from his as the new owner labored diligently to make her mark on the neighborhood.

His brow furrowed as he took in the sight; he had not been consulted about the incoming change in proprietors. The fact that he had been left out of the loop irritated him. Still, there was nothing he could do about it.

Frowning, he shook his head. His reflection in the glass returned a grimace.

"There she goes again."

Lowering his newspaper, his *daed* looked up. "There goes who?"

"Amity Schroder. You know—that *fraulein* who is opening the new store. She's got all sorts of people bringing in all sorts of gewgaws."

Daed thumbed through the rest of the news. "Don't see that it's any concern of yours. Better to have another business there rather than have it sitting empty. More customers are always welcome."

"I'd hoped to buy that side when it came up for sale. I wanted to knock down these walls in the middle and expand our seating space."

"I thought Charlotte Dekker's *familie* would give you that option. But it looks like Tanner had other ideas. Sold it right out from under you, didn't he?"

"*Ja.* Tanner promised he would give me first consideration after his *grossmammi* closed the quilt shop." Prickling with disappointment, Ethan turned away from the scene outside. Reaching for the dish towel draped over one shoulder, he then wiped his hands. "Guess he wasn't a man of his word."

"At least the new owner is Amish."

Ethan's frown deepened. "Not the sort I'd welcome as a neighbor."

"What's the matter with her?" The old man lowered his head, peering over the edge of thick black rims. "We've spoken a few times. She seems nice enough."

"I wouldn't be so sure about that. She's got a fresh mouth and likes to argue."

"Seems to me the girl's got grit." After clearing his gravelly throat, Wayne Zehr chuckled. "Maybe if you'd try smiling instead of snapping, she'd be a little friendlier."

Ethan declined to answer. He hadn't slept well the night before. His restless mind kept him tossing and turning. They'd only lived in Burr Oak for a few months. Everything was unfamiliar. The change had been hard, but necessary. Working day and night, he was determined to make the new venture a success. Fail, and he'd lose everything.

He rubbed his tired eyes, then glanced at the clock on the wall. Ten to six. The doors hadn't opened yet, but the day was already filled with activity. Plain folks rose before the sun to start work, and the vendors supplying the goods expected someone to be available as they made their rounds. Gemma Stutz had already dropped off the muffins and cinnamon rolls she baked fresh every day. Jonah Hoffman's butcher shop, too, had delivered the best cuts of deli meat.

And Dottie Weaver never failed to bring in loaves of her home-baked bread for the sandwiches served at lunchtime. In another hour, the morning rush would begin as people lined up to grab a hot drink and a quick breakfast before heading to work. He silently vowed to make his little corner café the best in town; customers had already begun to talk about the quality of his beverages and the comfort of his service.

He walked behind the counter. "Miss Schroder is nice enough, I'm sure," he said, flicking on the propane-powered appliances. "But she's too progressive for my tastes. Don't know if you saw it, but she's brought in a computer." As he spoke, his mind flitted back to the day he'd heard the retail space occupying the other half of the building had a new owner. Turned out in a blue frock, white apron, black hose and flats, the petite woman's outfit was simple but smartly worn. A white *kapp* covered her hair. Dark locks were pinned into a tight bun, but a few strands managed to escape. The curls brushed her intelligent brow, adding a glimmer of mischief to her youthful demeanor. She'd introduced herself right away. Full of energy and ideas, she smiled and laughed often.

She was also more than willing to stand up and speak her mind.

Not the way a lady should act at all.

"These Texas Amish do things we might not." A shrug rolled off his *daed's* shoulders. "Don't know if it's a bad thing. Just different."

Ethan sniffed with disapproval. "Back in Augsberger, Bishop Swarey would never have granted permission for the use of unnecessary electronics."

Daed folded his newspaper and set it aside. A monthly release, *Thrifty Living* featured a little bit of everything for the local Plain community—word-of-mouth news jawed over a neighbor's fence, at a livestock auction, or in a sewing circle. "We're not in Oklahoma anymore."

"Guess not."

"Since we live here now, it's up to us to adjust our ways."

"I get what you're saying. When in Rome, do as the Romans." Frustrated, he pressed out a sigh. "Not sure I'd agree."

"*Ach*, how is it I raised such a stick-in-the-mud? You sure took after your *mamm*. She always was too stiff and proper."

"Nothing wrong with that."

Daed shook his head. "I loved Letha, *Gott* rest her soul. But she'd have been a happier woman if she'd learned to bend. Compromise is part of getting along in life."

"I don't feel comfortable doing that. Not when it concerns things our *Ordnung* forbids."

"But theirs does not," *Daed* countered. "If you don't like it, petition the *Leit* to change it."

"I might do that." Mulling the idea, Ethan opened a canister. He scooped out a heap of whole-roasted *kaffee* beans, dumped them into a grinder and then cranked the handle until the remnants looked like coarse pepper. After pouring the grounds into a French press, he let the boiling water rest before adding it. Poured too hot, it would scorch the grounds and give the beverage a burned flavor.

Letting the grounds steep, he stirred them before placing the lid on the press. He pressed the plunger, pushing the blend down to the bottom of the carafe. The dark roast produced a rich brew. Created with raw beans from Costa Rica, the full-bodied brew was flavored with notes of cherry, honey and plum. He filled two cups and carried both to the café table where *Daed* sat.

"Better drink up. We'll be opening soon."

Leaning forward, Wayne inhaled the fragrant scent. "*Ach*, this is one of my better blends." He gulped down a mouthful. A master crafter, he drank his hot and black. Adding anything else to it was an insult.

Ethan took a chair. He added a splash of cream, preferring to smooth the acidity. Unlike other cafés that relied on prepackaged blends, the *kaffee* he served was roasted and freshly ground every morning.

"I'm beginning to wonder if it was a mistake moving to Texas," he said, unwilling to let the conversation drop. Burr Oak had a thriving Amish community, but their branch was a bit more permissive than he was accustomed to. Wary of worldly ideas and values, the Old Order settlement he was raised in kept *Englischers* at arm's length to preserve the community and its values. And the use of electricity was *verboten* unless provided by generators or other means not connected to the city power grid. Cell phones and computers were also given a wide berth.

"You weren't doing *gut*. You've struggled since Priscilla passed. So are Charity and Liam."

Dropping his gaze, Ethan stared into the depths of his cup. The words pulled at his heartstrings even as a sense of helplessness washed through him. Priscilla's sudden death had torn a gaping hole through their lives. Losing his *mamm* had turned their happy *sohn* into a sullen, angry teenager. Charity, too, had changed. Once a chatterbox, his daughter had grown quiet and uncommunicative.

Attempting to find a bit of warmth, his hands circled the stoneware mug. "I don't know what to do."

"I do. And you know it, too. You just won't admit it."

"The *youngies* need a *mutter*," he said, repeating the sentence he'd heard a thousand times before.

"Aye. And you need a wife."

"I'm not sure I'm ready. It's not even been a year…" Unable to go any further, he let his words drift off.

"Prissy belongs to the Lord," *Daed* said. "She is free from the sorrows of this world."

Ethan swallowed against the rush of emotion pulsing through him. Grief continued to be a millstone, grinding his psyche down to nothing. Watching his *ehefrau's* coffin as it was lowered into the cold ground had been a blow that had taken him to his knees.

"It's not fair. What about those left behind?" Clenching his fingers, he pressed his fist against his chest. "My heart has a hole bigger than my hand. How do I fill it when it feels so empty?"

Daed returned a gentle look. "It doesn't have to be. Cloaking yourself in grief—in the past—isn't what the Lord intends for us to do. Instead of weeping, rejoice that *Gott* has prepared a place for us in heaven."

Looking back, Ethan felt a tremble beneath his skin. Waves of memories crashed through his mind, each slamming in harder than the last. Barely eighteen when he'd married Priscilla, he'd imagined spending his life with her, raising their *youngies* as they transitioned into a ripe old age. He'd meant every word when they'd taken their vows. To love her. To cherish her. To protect her. But *Gott* hadn't seen fit to grant them much time together.

He managed a breath. And then another. "I don't feel any joy."

Daed shifted, placing a firm hand on his arm. "It's time to move on, *sohn*. You have to live again."

"I am trying." And he was. Desperately. But the agony tearing through him left him feeling vulnerable. Defenseless. How did a man recover from losing the love of his life? He wasn't sure. He'd never imagined his dear Priscilla would be the first to pass. She died after a bout with pneumonia. A delicate woman, she'd struggled for years with her health.

Daed leaned back. "It's hard, I know. But you need to think about Liam and Charity. Your *youngie*s need a woman in the *haus*." He stroked his long gray beard. A bit on the scraggly side, he only trimmed it twice a year, for Christmas and Easter. "A helpmeet would go a long way toward easing your burden."

Ethan blinked against the moisture blurring his vision. "Since I've no one to marry, I suppose I could hire a housekeeper."

Daed shook his head. A squint etched the edges of his eyes. "You could. But how long would that last? You are still a young man. And you want more *kinder. Ja?*"

"I do. Many more." He spread his hands in frustration. "But it's been a long time since I've courted. I wouldn't know where to begin."

"Why don't you start with letters? Some folks are shy and prefer to put their thoughts on paper before they meet in person." *Daed* tapped the newspaper with a finger. "In the socials section, there are *frauleins* requesting pen pals. That might be a nice way to meet a few ladies. You could start by exchanging notes and see how you like it."

"Nay," he said, brushing off the suggestion. "I prefer the old-fashioned way. In person." *Daed* was persistent when it came to the idea he needed to remarry right away. Of course, he'd like to. But he didn't want to rush into a relationship, either. When an Amish man settled on his helpmeet, it was for life. Choose the wrong woman and he'd be stuck.

"Suit yourself." *Daed* shook a finger. "But you need someone before this *familie* falls apart."

"I know…" He scrubbed a hand across his bearded face. As a widower, he was entitled to shave it off. But he couldn't. Not yet. He wasn't ready.

"Believe me when I say I only want what is best for you

and my *enkelkinder*." Offering a smile of encouragement, *Daed* put a hand on his arm. "Maybe you could sit down and try to write a letter. It doesn't have to be your whole life. Just reach out and say hello. It wouldn't hurt you to make a lady friend."

Ethan glanced at the newspaper. It wasn't uncommon for the Amish to do their courting through the mail. "I'll try." Not now, but maybe later. He'd never been much for putting his thoughts on paper.

The conversation thankfully didn't have a chance to go further.

Charity poked her head out of the kitchen. Now twelve, she was required to dress in a manner that wouldn't attract unwanted attention. Her ankle-length dress was cut from coarse gray fabric, as were her apron and head covering. Her prayer *kapp*, too, had subtle differences from those worn by the Burr Oak Amish. The style was more akin to a head-scarf, flat and unpleated. Loosely fitting around the head, it tucked up beneath her hair, hiding every tendril. Two strings tied under her chin held it securely in place.

"There's a man at the back door asking to come into the utility room."

Ethan froze. "Now, why would that be?"

"He said something about installing the broadband."

"I never ordered that." Leaving his *kaffee*, Ethan pushed away from the table. He rose and rounded the counter.

"I think he's here for the lady next door. I heard her talking to that *Englisch* fellow who works with her. He was saying he needed it installed for the stuff he was doing." More than a little excited, Charity grinned. "He said the whole building will have Wi-Fi."

Ethan bristled. Since claiming the keys to her side, Amity Schroder had been making changes to the property. Changes he didn't agree to. As tenants-in-common, each was supposed to have a fifty-fifty say on such matters. Rudely, she'd consulted him on nothing.

"I'll not allow the devil's contrivance to be installed."

"Don't think there's anything you can do," *Daed* called from behind.

Ethan's attention swung between his daughter and father. "We will see about that."

Raising his eyebrows, *Daed* shot back a quizzical look. A smile lingered around the upturned edges of his mouth. "Go with *Gott*." Chuckling, he plucked a pencil out of his pocket, then jotted a few letters on the crossword puzzle.

Spurred into action, Ethan stomped through the kitchen toward the back alley. A service tech in a brown uniform waited by a large white van. Clipboard in hand, the man had come prepared to do his job.

Not going to happen. If Amity Schroder wanted an argument, then she would have one.

Hands on her hips, Amity Schroder surveyed her new shop. The retail space she'd recently purchased was still in disarray. Now that the display cases and other shelving had arrived, merchandise needed to be unpacked. Up with the sun, her staff was hard at work.

Blowing out a breath, she brushed a few stray curls away from her face. When she'd opened her booth at the local farmer's market, she'd never envisioned her hobby would grow into a proper business. Seeking a way to make a little pin money, she'd peddled things the ranch produced in abundance—fresh honey from the beehives and holistic teas made from plants she grew herself. She also made potpourri and other items such as soaps and skin ointments. Within hours, she'd sold every item. That day, Amity's Amish Amenities was born.

Five years had passed in the blink of an eye. Saving every penny earned, she'd invested in a permanent location. Searching high and low, she'd finally found the perfect storefront. Some of the things she liked about the building were its charming brick facade, overhanging awning and large open bay windows. The design harkened back to a bygone era, when people were more accustomed to strolling on foot. Large rectangular picture windows overlooked the shared foyer from both sides. There were also two apartments on the second floor, which made the property worth investing in. Built by Amish craftsmen, it was cleverly powered by solar and propane.

Grateful, she sent up a quick prayer. "*Danke, Gott,* for leading me here."

With the Lord's help and hard work, she'd found her niche. No longer a one-woman operation, her staff included two shopgirls. She'd also hired an *Englisch* tech to design and manage her new website. Shoppers often inquired about ordering online. It only made sense to offer the opportunity. She'd also branched out into consignment work, giving other Amish women a place to sell their crafts.

A sudden sharp bang interrupted.

"You in there," a deep male voice called.

Startled, Amity turned toward the entrance. Expecting a serviceman, she'd left the foyer entrance unlocked.

Recognizing the intruder, she winced. Dressed in traditional Amish clothes covered by a denim apron, the man's electric blue eyes snapped above a fierce frown. Dark curls blended into his sideburns and beard.

Ach, *not this fellow again.*

Heart thudding, Amity forced herself to stay calm. For

all the advantages the location offered, the only bad thing was the owner of the *kaffeehaus*. The real estate agent who'd handled the transaction assured her the proprietor of the neighboring retail space was a Plain *familie* man.

Only part of that was true.

He was Amish.

He was also as cantankerous as an old mule.

A tall man in his early thirties, Ethan Zehr was the most disagreeable person she'd ever had the misfortune to deal with. Since the day she'd acquired the keys to her half, he'd made it a point to argue over every detail. He didn't seem to like anything about her.

Determined not to be ignored, Ethan banged harder. "Open up!"

"It's not locked." She made a motion with her hand indicating that he should enter. "Come in."

The bell jingled as he pushed open the door. Without offering a proper morning greeting, he launched straight into his complaint.

"There's a man in the alley with a van," he sputtered. "He says he's here to install the internet."

"*Ja.* I ordered it. As soon as it's set up, there will be internet access for our customers."

Snorting with disapproval, his direct gaze never wavered. "You'll do no such thing."

Amity barely stopped herself from rolling her eyes. She'd already dealt with Ethan more than she cared to. As far as he was concerned, not a thing she did was proper.

"I need it," she said simply.

"The internet is not a need. It is a want," he corrected, staring down the bridge of his nose with disapproval. "Or have you forgotten the Bible warns against desires that can lead us astray."

Lacing her hands together, Amity forced herself to maintain a civil tone. *Gott* also counseled that one should love their enemy. But she was finding it extremely difficult to tolerate him.

"It isn't for my personal use. The *Ordnung* states we may install such utilities for our *Englisch* employees to use," she explained, gesturing toward the computer sitting on the counter. New in the box, it had yet to be unpacked. "The young man I hired needs it for his job."

Nostrils flaring, Ethan surveyed the offending machine. "This is not acceptable. At all." Having had his say, he crossed his arms.

Amity crossed her own and held her place. While her stature wasn't any match for his superior height, she was determined to stand up for herself. Ethan was doing everything in his power to ruffle her feathers. Holding himself as a standard bearer was one thing. But attacking her character when she'd done nothing wrong was quite another. As one baptized in the church, she'd pledged her life to serve *Gott*, her *familie* and her *gemeinschaft*.

"There is no reason for you to be argumentative. Perhaps it would ease your mind to speak to Bishop Harrison. I am sure he would be happy to clarify matters."

Expression tightening, he shot her a narrow look. "Oh, you can guarantee I'll be speaking with the bishop. This very morning if I can arrange it."

"Please do."

His eyebrows shot up. "You've quite the confidence."

"I speak for myself and in my defense." Her legs quivered beneath her weight, but she had no intention of backing down.

An awkward pause passed between them.

Frown deepening, he cleared his throat. "Then it's settled."

Stomping toward the door, he threw back a final warning. "I've sent the serviceman away. There will be nothing more done until the matter is clarified."

That said, he left.

Staring in his wake, Amity released her pent-up breath. Folks like Ethan made it hard to turn the other cheek. Since the meters and wiring needed to install the Wi-Fi were on his side of the property, he had the upper hand.

Shaking her head, she pressed a hand against her middle. Her stomach was a mass of knots and nerves. Arguing wasn't the best way to begin the day, but she was determined not to let Ethan's resistance deter her plans. Anxious and behind schedule, she had a lot to do. His visit had only served to waste time. The days were ticking away.

"Lord, keep me grounded," she murmured. If she hadn't known better, she'd have sworn he was one of the Ely's Bluff Amish. Taciturn and aloof, they'd recently begun integrating into the Burr Oak congregation after the passing of their elderly bishop. Fiercely resistant to change, they were reluctant to embrace any sort of technology. The differing outlooks often led to a clash of values.

She didn't doubt Ethan meant to do everything he said. If a complaint against another was made, the offender would be summoned to explain. Handing out disciplinary actions to those who strayed from acceptable behavior was only one of the bishop's many duties.

It didn't worry her that she might be judged out of compliance. She'd already consulted Bishop Harrison and received permission to proceed. If Ethan wanted to take a fool out of himself…well, that was his concern.

Determined not to let his complaints rattle her, Amity blew out a breath.

The man's impossible. How will we ever get along?

Chapter Two

Unrolling a bolt of material across her worktable, Amity measured out the length. A linen stonewash in pale oyster, it was perfect for the valances and curtains she planned to make. Referring to the measurements she'd taken, she pinned the hems into place. Once she had the desired shape, a quick bit of stitching would bring it all together.

Humming to a gospel tune playing on the radio, she took a seat in front of a treadle sewing machine. Powered by foot, the vintage appliance sprang to life. The needle bobbed up and down in a steady rhythm. Passed down through several generations, it was a treasure she'd claimed after her *mamm* passed away.

Lost in her favorite activity, the hours disappeared.

"Amity?" A tap followed. "Did you hear me?"

She glanced up to see Rebecca standing at the door. Tall and spare, with rosy cheeks and freckles, her *schwester* was clad in a sunny yellow frock covered by a neat white apron. Her thick chestnut hair was tucked primly beneath her prayer *kapp*. A few wisps had managed to escape, teasingly framing her face, adding a touch of playfulness to her stern appearance.

"*Ach*, sorry. I was lost in my sewing. Did you need something?"

Rebecca stepped inside. "I heard you working and wondered if you'd gotten to my dress." Newly engaged, her *schwester* would soon be married.

Amity grinned. "*Ja.* I've got it cut out and tacked up." Rising, she pulled a dressmaker's dummy out of its corner. While it was customary for Amish brides to make their dresses and those of their bridesmaids, Rebecca had asked for help in picking the material and shades. To conceal her work, Amity kept it covered until she was ready to show it. She tugged off the sheet.

"What do you think?"

Rebecca blinked back tears. "Oh, my. It's beautiful."

"You like it?" The design was simple, but striking. What made it stand out was the color. For the bride's dress, she'd chosen a shade of blue. A white cape and apron would add the finishing touches. She'd planned to have Rebecca try it on that very day but had gotten sidetracked.

"I do." Gaze shining, Rebecca added, "I can't believe I'll be Mrs. Caleb Sutter in a few weeks."

"I know *Gott* brought you two together."

"I'm still pinching myself that my *Englisch* doctor had some Amish in him."

Amity chuckled. "Coincidence is the Lord's way of remaining anonymous." Adopted at birth, Caleb Sutter's search for his identity had revealed quite a surprise twist. His *mutter* was a Plain woman. Attempting to conceal the shame of a pregnancy out of wedlock, she'd secretly given up her newborn *sohn*. Learning the truth, Caleb had embraced his heritage and gotten baptized.

Rebecca swept the tips of her fingers over the soft fabric. "You'll be next, I bet."

"*Ach*, I doubt that. Seems every man I walkabout with turns out to be Mr. Wrong."

"That's because they're Mr. Wrong For You."

"I've begun to think the Lord meant for me to be alone."

"That's not true. *Gott* will send the right man when it's time."

"At my age, I'm firmly a spinster. I should get a cat. Or maybe two. That will give me something to cuddle." Now twenty-five, the best years of her life were frittering away.

"Give up now and you'll find no one. Why don't you talk to Lisl Kleinhoffer? She's made some *gut* matches."

Amity grimaced. The last date Lisl arranged for her was a disaster. Trying one last time, she'd renewed her ad in the paper for a new pen pal. So far, no replies. "I'm not really in the mood to think kind thoughts about men and their ways," she huffed. "Especially since the one next door is so difficult."

"I'll take that to mean Mr. Zehr is still giving you problems?"

"Aye. He is." As she spoke, a flash of icy blue eyes belonging to a bearded face flashed through her mind. Ethan Zehr was ruggedly handsome, and his direct gaze never failed to send a shiver down her spine. Since they'd begun to clash, he was on her mind night and day. It bothered her he'd managed to work his way into her life in such an unwelcome manner.

Arched eyebrows shot high. "What's he done now?"

Amity placed her hands on her hips. Indignation straightened her shoulders. "He's complained to Bishop Harrison about the internet service I want to install."

"Why is he complaining? It is permitted."

"I know. But he doesn't see a reason to have it."

"Doesn't make sense. Does he not know our *Ordnung* allows it?"

"That's exactly what I intend to say at the meeting tomorrow," she answered without hesitation. "Mr. Zehr might come from a stricter brethren, but that's no reason to bully the rest of us. I intend to stand up and defend myself."

"I agree—you should. It's a shame you have to share ownership of the building. It is too bad he was there first."

"If the location and price weren't so reasonable, I'd have passed it by. And it does have the walk-up above. The apartment is perfect for one. Can't beat that."

Rebecca shook her head. "I can't believe you're moving."

"*Ja.* I am. Levi and Gail need the room. And it makes more sense to be in town since getting there can be so difficult in the winter. If I live above the shop, all I have to do is walk downstairs in the morning to open up."

"Are you sure you want to do that? Aren't Mr. Zehr and his *familie* also living on their side?"

"They are. But I don't think they'll be there much longer. His *daed*—his name is Wayne, and he is quite nice by the way—mentioned he'd like a *haus* in the country. Somewhere they could have livestock and horses. He thinks it would be *gut* for his *enkelkinder*, too. From the bits and pieces I've picked up in conversation, Ethan's *sohn* is running with the wrong sort and getting in trouble."

"Correct me if I am wrong, but didn't you say Mr. Zehr is a widower?"

"Aye. I believe Ethan's *ehefrau* passed almost a year ago."

"How sad. I imagine the loss is still very hard on him."

"His *tochter*, too. Charity, bless her heart, is such a sweet girl."

"Oh? How old is she?"

"Twelve." Amity shook her head. "The poor child is starved for attention. Give her a kind word and she lights up. When she's not working at the *kaffeeshop*, she loves coming over and visiting with Sophie and Emily. Her *daed* has told her not to be a bother, but that's not stopped her. I get the feeling she is doing her best to be a grown-up, but she's struggling."

Rebecca's gaze grew distant with memory. "I remember how hard it was on Gail when *Mamm* passed and she had the three of us to look after."

Amity's throat tightened as a wave of sadness rippled through her. She'd barely turned thirteen when her *mamm* died from cancer. As the eldest, Gail had stepped in. Eight years later, their *daed* had suddenly died from a heart attack. He'd also left behind a large cattle ranch…and four girls who had no idea how to run it.

"*Ja*, we've both stood in Charity's place."

"I'll pray for healing in their *familie*. I'll also pray you and Mr. Zehr can settle your differences."

Amity rolled her eyes. "That would truly be wonderful."

"The Lord does sometimes work in mysterious ways." Smiling, Rebecca pulled her in for a quick hug. "Since you've got things on your mind, don't worry about my dress. We can manage it some other time."

"If you will give me another hour, we can do it before supper."

"Really?"

"Of course. It won't take but a minute for me to check the sizing." Eyeing her sibling from head to foot, she gave a disapproving frown. "You've not a spare ounce on you, so stop losing weight."

Rebecca's expression briefly twisted. "I've been so worried Caleb will change his mind that I can barely eat a bite. Like Noel did. He was so angry when he found out I couldn't have *kinder*. I've never been so humiliated."

"Noel was a fool. You were fortunate he called off the engagement," Amity said, offering a steadying hand. "Caleb isn't going anywhere. He loves you just the way you are."

A voice sounded, breaking into the conversation.

"Girls, are you here?" Gail called out.

"We're in the sewing room," Rebecca answered back.

Baby on one hip and a four-year-old gamboling in her wake, Gail entered. "Can one of you help with the *kinder*? I'm about to start supper and could use extra hands."

Sammy squealed, running to pump the treadle on the sewing machine. "Big thing!"

Amity bent and lifted him away. "No, no! That's not for play."

"Nein, Tante, nein!" Sammy kicked in protest. Curious and active, he was constantly on the move.

"Sorry," Gail apologized behind a tired smile. Apron stained and dress torn at the hem, her *kapp* was comically askew. She looked as if she'd been run through the wringer and hung out to dry. "He's been into everything today. I couldn't even get him down for a nap."

"It's no problem." Amity set Sammy on his feet. "I could have used him an hour ago when my legs were getting tired."

Without missing a beat, Sammy snatched a length of measuring tape, flicking it in the air. "I'm ropin' moos!" he exclaimed, pretending to lasso an imaginary cow.

"He wants to be a cowboy like his *daed*," Gail said, eyeing her energetic *youngie*. "As soon as he turns five, Levi's going to teach him to ride."

Amity gave her nephew a fond look. "He's growing so fast." She glanced at the rosy-cheeked toddler in Gail's arms. "They both are."

"Levi's already talking about another. Imagine us with four."

"Will there be?" she asked, eyeing Gail's waist.

"Too early to know. I'm just saying the Lord might see fit to bless us again." Chuckling, Gail added, "But let's not worry about that. It's Rebecca's time now." Her gaze swept over the dress. "You've done such a lovely job."

"I can't wait to try it on," Rebecca said.

Aware time was getting away, Amity made a shooing motion. "Go and help with the little ones." She reclaimed her measuring tape. Sammy whined in protest but let it go. "We'll do your fitting this evening."

"I do need to get supper started." Gail headed toward the door. "You coming, Rebecca?"

"*Ja.* I am."

Left to herself, Amity circled the dressmaker's dummy. Adjusting a few straight pins, she smoothed stray wrinkles out of the soft fabric. Making a wedding dress was always a joyful occasion—a symbol of the hopes and dreams a bride had for her future.

An unexpected rush of emotion blurred her vision. Emptiness gnawed her heart. Although she longed to meet someone, romance had always eluded her. Most of that was because she had a habit of speaking her mind. Saying what she believed and refusing to back down had given her the reputation of being difficult. And while most Amish men valued a helpmeet who could manage a large *familie* and household with a firm hand, they also expected their wives to present a modest face in public.

"Always a bridesmaid," she murmured. "Never a bride."

"I do not quarrel with making an honest living," Ethan said, closing his argument. "But I do not see the need to use the internet to do so. In my opinion, it's like opening the door and letting the devil walk in."

Bishop Harrison nodded gravely. "I understand your concerns. However, our *Ordnung* does allow the use of electricity and internet for business purposes." Adorned with simple furnishings, the walls of his office were lined with shelves filled with worn books. A wise and respected elder, he sat in a sturdy oak chair, his weathered hands folded in his lap.

Unwilling to compromise, Ethan kept going. "I don't understand why it's needed," he grumbled, glancing toward Amity. "All she sells is knickknacks. Nothing of any importance."

"That's not true," she said without waiting for her turn to speak.

Bishop Harrison immediately held up a hand. His stern expression never wavered. "I've heard your argument, Amity. Ethan deserves his rebuttal."

Brushing a hand across his mouth, Ethan glanced toward his antagonist. It had taken an entire day to get a meeting with Bishop Harrison to file his complaint. And yet another day had to pass before a hearing could be arranged. Through the last two days, Amity had continued working in her shop. At least she'd removed the new computer, whisking it out of sight. He'd peered through her storefront window after she'd closed and had been somewhat mollified to see a vintage cash register sitting on the counter.

Having brought the matter this far, he had no intention of backing down. And he certainly wouldn't let Amity Schroder's infectious grin and the adorable dimple at the corner of her mouth persuade him into changing his mind.

"As Mr. Zehr was told, I'm having the internet installed," Amity said, taking her turn to speak. "I've had a website designed, and I expect to be taking orders online. This requires a computer and the ability to process credit card payments. And as many other places do in town, I plan to offer free Wi-Fi, too."

"I don't agree to having it," he countered sourly. "The

more technology allowed, the greater the threat to the integrity of our community."

"I understand your concern," she allowed. "But I am not using these things myself. I have an *Englisch boi* to handle online communications and order fulfillment. He will work in the back office. As for my Amish employees, they have the tools they need to work comfortably without violating their beliefs."

"It is a fine line to walk," Bishop Harrison interjected. "However, the Lord does say the plans of the diligent lead to abundance."

"Abundance in Satan's playground holds no attraction to me," Ethan countered.

Adjusting his weight in his chair, the church elder leaned forward. "I appreciate things might be different where you come from. But I assure you the *Leit* here gives new technologies every due consideration before we amend our *Ordnung*. First and foremost, we consider the social ramifications and how it affects our members. Yes, the internet can be abused. But it can also be a tool. And like any tool, it is to be used with common sense and care."

"For myself, I have no use of it," Amity added. "I don't carry a cell phone, nor do I care to use one. But having these things for my shop will help keep my doors open. That, in turn, allows me to keep members of our community employed."

Bishop Harrison spread his hands. "You both present valid arguments. And I am inclined to err on the side of caution."

Sure he was about to strike a blow, Ethan nodded with satisfaction.

Amity's confidence wavered. "But—"

Bishop Harrison held up a hand. "But as much as we might not care to admit it, the world will keep changing around us."

Pausing, his gaze swept between them but focused on neither. "It might be all right to maintain a distance from technology but isolating ourselves in ignorance would be foolish and foolhardy. I judge that Amity may proceed."

She grinned. "I appreciate that, Bishop."

Bishop Harrison gave her a sharp glance. "Boast not lest you show arrogance," he warned. "The *Ordnung* allows you liberty, but do not abuse it. You are headstrong, Amity, and often invite criticism."

She dropped her gaze. "*Ja.* I understand."

"I have no other say?" Ethan asked.

"*Nein.* The matter is closed," the bishop said.

Stomach turning to knots, Ethan swallowed hard. So that was that. He'd lost. She'd won. Failure rankled him, but he had no other route of appeal within the church hierarchy. Once the bishop announced a decision, his was the final word.

"I believe you are remiss in your decision, but I will abide."

Bishop Harrison made a few notes on a legal pad. "Duly noted. I'll also add that you are not being forced to use the internet, nor are your customers." Placing a hand on his Bible, he continued, "It is my recommendation you read what the Lord has to say in Thessalonians about minding your affairs. I believe you might find it enlightening."

Called out, Ethan acknowledged the rebuke. Stuck in his narrow point of view, he'd failed to acknowledge that he might be on the wrong side of the matter.

He rose and put on his hat. "Your words are well taken, Bishop," he said. "*Danke* for your time. I'll bid you both *guter tag* and take my leave."

Scurrying out of the office, he headed outside. "Can't believe I did that," he muttered to no one in particular. "Arguing with the woman over nothing that affects me."

The realization was a bitter pill to swallow. The weight of his actions burdened his conscience. It all came down to the fact that Tanner Dekker had gone back on his word. Tanner knew he'd wanted to take full ownership of the building and would pay to acquire it. They'd even agreed on a tentative price. And then things had gone silent. A few weeks later, the new owner walked in to introduce herself. He didn't know what Amity Schroder had done to weasel him out, but the fact that Tanner didn't give him the opportunity to make a counteroffer was upsetting. Losing the purchase, he'd done everything in his power to hinder Amity's plans. Bishop Harrison could have rightly pointed out several passages about treating one's neighbor fairly.

Ethan glanced toward the clear sky. *I'll do better, Lord. Bear with me as I get through this. I may be slow, but I'll catch up.* True piety was not in resisting the currents of change but in navigating them with humility and grace. The path was a difficult one. But he would persist. One step at a time.

Life in Burr Oak was different. The Texas Amish had their way of doing things. The fact they had a dedicated church building was one example. In other Amish communities, Sunday worship was hosted by congregants in their homes on a rotating basis. Burr Oak, however, was spread out across the rural countryside. Most Plain folks lived on farms and ranches far outside the city limits. Coming into a central location in town was easier than traveling miles to reach a neighbor.

Heading down the sidewalk, Ethan left the church behind. Respecting *Gott's* handiwork, the original Amish settlers kept much of the natural terrain intact. Built on a gently sloping knoll bracketed by trees and other flora, the simple white-washed structure was a short walk from the town square.

Part of the original settlement, Main Street was still paved with cobblestones. Sturdy trees lined the sidewalks, offering a sheltered place for folks to walk as they browsed the offerings from local merchants. Directly behind the shops was a stretch of acreage that served as the city park. The overall effect offered visitors a unique glimpse of the American frontier during the early days of settlement.

It was hard not to notice the *Englisch* tourists. With smartphones in hand, many snapped pictures and videos of the Amish as they went about their day. Most of the Plain folks ignored the intrusive lens. Whether they liked it or not, technology had crept into their way of life.

Slipping a hand into his pocket, he checked his watch. Ten after nine. The early meeting had thrown him off schedule. The morning hours were typically the busiest at the café.

Picking up his steps, he turned down the narrow alley that led into the back of his shop. Though the building shared a single front entrance, the rear had two separate ones. Each vendor could come and go without disturbing the other. Actively shopping for a large *haus* on a few nice acres, his plans included renting the apartment above for extra income.

After walking into the kitchen, Ethan hung up his hat and snagged a work apron. He pushed back his hair, then washed his hands and stepped into his busy day.

Daed was working behind the counter, putting together a ham and cheese on rye. After wrapping and sacking it, he added a small bag of chips and a chocolate muffin.

Charity stood at the *kaffee* station. The scent of the rich dark espresso filled the air. Along with the traditional offerings of regular and decaf, the whirring machine delivered a steady stream of custom beverages. Brow furrowed with concentration, she crafted each order with care. Having worked since she was knee-high, Charity was an experienced barista.

She could mix mocha cappuccinos and caramel macchiatos without blinking an eye.

Another customer stepped up to the counter. And then another. The orders kept coming.

Ethan cut a glance to the sacks lining a shelf, waiting to be delivered.

"Where's Liam?"

Daed shrugged. "He left about half an hour ago and hasn't come back."

Ethan frowned. It wasn't like the *boi* was on foot. For his fifteenth birthday, he'd been gifted with a bicycle. So Liam could deliver several orders at one time, his bicycle was outfitted with a basket and pannier bags.

"He's off fooling around again," he muttered when customers were out of earshot. "Can't depend on him." Keeping a job was something Liam didn't seem interested in doing. Since leaving school at fourteen, as most Amish did, he'd gotten a chip on his shoulder. Now, at an age when a young man should be focusing on a trade that would make him a living, the teenager had shown no proclivity for work.

The alley door leading into the kitchen opened.

Liam strolled in. Moving with lanky grace, he plucked a plastic bottle out of a nearby cooler.

Leaving the front, Ethan headed to confront him. "Where have you been?"

Gulping a mouthful of water, Liam dragged his hand across his lips. "Chill, Pops," he said, using the slang he'd picked up from *Englisch* boys. "I'm on it."

"I am not your 'Pops.' Nor will you speak to me in such a manner."

"Whatever." A shrug rolled off Liam's narrow shoulders. Tall but thin, he already stood near Ethan's height. When he matured and filled out, he'd be a powerful man.

"Orders are waiting. People would like to have their food delivered."

"Just stopped for a break, is all," Liam mumbled back.

Ethan drew in a breath. It wasn't hard to guess what the break was all about. A cloyingly acrid smell clung to the teen's clothes. "I've warned you about smoking."

Liam returned a narrow gaze. "So what? I took a quick break." Bottom lip protruding, he spouted in a nasty tone, "It's not like you can stop me, or anything like that."

"If you won't mind me, think of your *mamm*. Your disrespect would break her heart."

Hands turning to fists, Liam's stance crackled with tension. "She isn't here to care, is she?"

Ethan inwardly winced. The verbal lash cut deep, reopening a wound barely healed. The accusation was a vicious one. "We will talk later," he returned stiffly. "These orders need to be delivered. Now."

"Nein." Liam's voice grew louder, attracting the attention of customers. The entrance separating the kitchen and counter area was wide open. Curious looks were beginning to drift their way. "I'm not doing it. I quit."

"If you want a roof over your head and food in your belly, you'll do your job."

Chin set in a stubborn line, Liam's expression turned into a sneer. "I hate this place," he snapped. "And I hate this job. I'm not doing it anymore!" Stomping outside, he disappeared back into the alley.

Shocked into silence, Ethan regretfully shook his head. Moody, sullen and scowling, Liam seemed determined to push everyone away.

Heart thudding hollowly, he pressed the tips of his fingers to his aching temple. Worn and grieving, he was doing his best to salvage their lives. Stumbling, he was close to falling.

Close to failure. How could he help Liam through his grief when he'd barely dealt with his own? Robbed of his authority by his *sohn's* attitude, there was nothing he could do to stop Liam from going down the wrong path. Smoking was only the tip of the iceberg. He did not doubt that more trouble was waiting around the corner.

Control slipping through his fingers, he sent up a desperate prayer.

Lord, please lay Your hand over Liam before he does something he'll regret.

Chapter Three

"Excuse me, sir. What's the password to the Wi-Fi?"

Ethan frowned at the woman who'd asked the question. She was an *Englischer*, and her smartphone was firmly welded in her hand. "I'm sorry. We don't offer that here."

She gestured toward the entrance. "It says outside you have free internet."

"Aye, it belongs to the business next door."

The customer returned a peevish look. "Can't I use it here?"

Standing nearby, Charity cocked her head. "The password is 'welcome,'" she said, pausing from her work bussing tables.

The woman tapped at the screen. "That's what I needed. Thanks." After claiming her muffin and espresso, she slid into a nearby booth and began to scroll through her phone.

Ethan still didn't understand the hold the devices had on folks. Amity had gone ahead with her plans, and the service. Accepting that she had the right to offer it to her customers didn't mean his had to take advantage of it. But they did. In droves.

Perched on a stool nearby, *Daed* glanced up. "It's not been a bad thing," he commented. "Maybe you haven't noticed, but business has tripled."

It was true. Almost every table was occupied. People needing a break from the office worked on laptops or tablets. Others texted on their phones. The longer they sat, the more they spent. By the end of the day, almost every edible item on the menu had been sold and devoured.

Shaking his head, Ethan rubbed his eyes. "I don't understand the attraction, but people seem to want it."

"It also helps spread *Gott's* word," *Daed* reminded him. "The Lord says we are to proclaim the gospel to all. There's nothing that says we can't send it out with a *gut tasse kaffee*."

Ethan's gaze traveled to the plaque hung above the door. His father had fashioned it himself, carefully cutting and sanding down the wood before burning the letters into its face: *Fellowship Kaffeehaus*, it read in a neat block script. *We Practice the Lord's Hospitality.*

"I suppose you're right."

"I've talked to that fella working for Amity," *Daed* continued. "After he went over it, it does make sense to have it."

"Like how?"

Taking advantage of the lull, *Daed* was jotting a few things in a small notebook he kept handy. Usually, it was to keep track of things he wanted to remember. "Well, those folks you see sitting here now are most likely texting their friends. They share pictures where they are, too."

"People do that?"

Carrying a tub full of paper plates and other debris, Charity dumped it in a trash bin behind the counter. "One lady told me she had over a thousand followers on her social media." Smiling shyly, she added, "She showed me the pictures she took. There's one of *Poppi* and me."

Ethan looked between the two. "There are pictures of you on the internet?"

Charity nodded. So did *Daed*. "I look pretty *gut* if I do say so myself," he said and grinned.

Ethan's eyebrows rose. Generally, the Amish did not welcome or encourage photographs. The Lord warned against creating any sort of graven images. Most Plain folks didn't make or display such items. Nevertheless, tourists persisted. "Can't say that I care for that." Doing business in the modern world meant sacrificing parts of their privacy to prying eyes.

As always, *Daed* took things in stride. "It's something our customers want, so we might as well let them have it," he said. "And since we benefit from the free advertising, we should pay half the bill."

"You expect me to pay for something I didn't want?"

"*Ja. Gott* commands we are not to deal unfairly with one another." Pushing his heavy frames back into place, the old man gave him a knowing look. "You should also ask her forgiveness. Being such a stubborn fool, you made a fuss over nothing."

Heat crept into Ethan's face. He gave himself another mental kick. Admitting he was wrong was hard. But being a decent human meant stepping up and owning his mistakes. He owed Amity an olive branch. "I suppose I should."

"You've not congratulated her on her opening. It wouldn't hurt you to bring her some *kaffee und dänisch* and wish her well."

"I could do that."

"Then do."

Ethan looked around. The clock had edged past one, signaling an end to the lunch hour. A few stragglers remained. "I can't go now. Liam's not back."

"The *boi* will show up. I'll mind the counter while you and Charity walk over."

Now or never. He doubted Amity would welcome his face, but he intended to man up and do the right thing. "All right. We'll only be a few minutes." Reaching for a stack of to-go cups, he looked to Charity. "Pack some cinnamon rolls and apple fritters. A half dozen of each."

Prepared to make things right, Ethan straightened his shoulders. Served a helping of crow, it was time to pick the feathers out of his teeth. It was also a humbling reminder from the Lord not to let arrogance come from his mouth.

He opened the door and stepped into the foyer. Allowing access to both shops, the reception area also hosted the public restrooms. Each owner had responsibility for its upkeep. To make the space more inviting, Amity and her shopgirls created a cute display. A couple of rocking chairs, matching side tables and quaint metal lamps offered a welcoming touch. Carefully crafted needlepoint canvasses with Biblical quotes had been hung on the walls. To accommodate the overflow from his shop, she'd also added tables and chairs. Baskets of scented potpourri and tea light candles sat atop lace doilies. Hand-carved wooden trays held other sundry items. She'd done it on her own and at her cost. All in all, the entryway had a blended look, merging into a cohesive whole. The decor gave the impression the two shops belonged together.

She has a gut *eye*, he thought. *She knows how to welcome the public.*

Blowing out a breath, he crossed to her shop. The bell above the door sent out a merry tinkle as he stepped into her territory.

Amity was hard at work. Swiping a duster across a shelf, she glanced up. "Can I help you, Mr. Zehr?"

Ethan cleared his throat. Her posture was one of defense. He'd given her trouble in the past, and she expected no less today. Nearby, a couple of shopgirls gave him a wary glance. Pointing, one whispered behind her hand to the other. The tension was thick enough to cut with a knife.

"I came to congratulate you on your opening," he said,

holding out the drink carrier. "There's *kaffee* and rolls for you and your staff." Offering a stiff nod, he added, "I hope you will enjoy them."

Amity's cautious smile brightened. "Why, that's so thoughtful of you. *Danke*. No one has had time to get a bite to eat all day. It will be most appreciated."

"You've been busy?"

"*Ja*. Very."

"Your shop is so pretty," Charity blurted.

Amity's eyes lit up. "Do you like it?"

"Oh, I do."

Ethan liked it, too. And he couldn't stop staring. Before she'd taken ownership, the place was shabby. Formerly a quilt shop, the elderly proprietor had allowed the inside to fall to ruin. Though the area was neat, no regular maintenance had been done for decades. The ceiling had tiles discolored by a leak from the plumbing above. The trickling dampness had caused the off-white paint to peel away from the walls. The wooden trim along the floor had also taken on rot.

He'd resented losing half the building to another merchant. Jealousy had seeded his heart as he'd watched Amity make the improvements. Overseeing a competent crew of Amish carpenters, she'd completely transformed the place. Damages repaired, she'd decorated in the style of an old-country mercantile. To evoke the ambiance of a bygone era, battery-powered lanterns lit the interior. Almost every product she sold was homemade, organic or all-natural.

"You've done a fine job. I'm impressed."

Amity pressed her hands together as if in prayer. "I put it in the Lord's hands. I couldn't have done any of it without His guidance."

Ethan nodded. The more he saw, the faster shadows of doubt slithered away. By her words and actions, Amity had proven she was intent on keeping her business a traditional one. As promised, he saw no signs of the offending computer. The credit card machine by the register was subtle and unobtrusive.

"I'll pray you are blessed with much success," he said, setting the cup holder on the counter. "Come, have some *kaffee* before it gets cold."

Amity beckoned for the shopgirls to join her. Each plucked out a cup. Opening the lid, one inhaled the fragrant brew. "I've been needing a hot drink."

Charity joined them. "We bought sweets, too."

Amity peeked inside the box. "Oh, my favorite. I love apple fritters."

A lanky young man ambled out of the back office. A curtain of dark bangs ruled over a pair of thick glasses. A pencil was tucked behind one ear. Dressed in slacks, a white shirt and loafers, he presented a sour look.

"Please don't tell me you severed the wiring to the broadband," he said behind a frown.

Amity backed him off. "Noah, please. You'll greet Mr. Zehr with respect. Any complaints he has, he will bring to me."

Ethan nervously cleared his throat. "I do have a matter to speak with you about."

Amity let the lid on the box drop. "Oh?"

Fearing she'd order him to leave, Ethan blurted out, "I'd like to pay half the internet bill."

Arched eyebrows rose. "What? Really?"

Guilt pinged. He'd been so focused on bringing her down that he didn't realize she would be the one to lift him. *"Ja."*

"Wow. Wasn't expecting that," Noah said.

Waving off her tech worker, Amity gave a kind smile. "I appreciate the offer, but it's not necessary. I wanted the service. I'll pay for it."

Ethan held firm. Admitting he was wrong was tough, but he was committed to following through. "My customers are using it, too. It isn't fair to take advantage without contributing to the cost."

Jaws dropped as everyone gawked. A few gasped loudly.

Aware that he'd have to insist, Ethan gathered his nerve to keep going. But he never had the chance. The bell above the door tinkled again. A tall dark-haired man dressed in a sheriff's uniform strode in. The cop's commanding presence brought an immediate halt to all conversation.

"Afternoon, folks," the officer said, tipping his white Stetson. "The old fella next door said I'd find Ethan Zehr here."

Ethan stepped forward. "That would be me."

"The name's Miller," the cop said by way of an introduction. "Is Liam Zehr your son?"

Ethan couldn't think of any reason an *Englisch* lawman would be looking for him. The Amish preferred to keep their business to themselves, rarely involving themselves with law enforcement. "*Ja.* He is." Cutting a glance to Charity, he saw fright drain the color from her face.

"*Datt...*" Crossing her arms to shield herself, Charity visibly shivered.

Amity protectively drew the youngster to one side. "Hush, child," she soothed in a calm tone. "Let the men talk."

Ethan's stomach tightened into knots. Breathing a quick prayer, he tried to keep calm. "What's going on?" After their argument, Liam had grudgingly returned to resume his duties. The last few days had been tense, but tolerable.

Now everything threatened to fall apart again. A thousand images flashed through his mind, none of them good. Liam was out on his bicycle. What if he had been hit by a car? Or worse...

The sheriff grimaced, jerking a thumb over one shoulder.

"I'm going to need you to come with me," he drawled. "Got your kid and a few of his friends sitting in the county jail."

Amity had planned for a quiet evening, but it didn't quite work out that way. The sound of a fierce argument filled the air. Shouting voices penetrated the walls separating her living quarters from the suite next door. The accusations, most of which came from the mouth of an angry teenage boy, were sharp and hurtful.

Shocked by the ugly words, she stepped off her stool. She hadn't meant to eavesdrop on the argument but could hardly avoid it. The battle commenced the moment Ethan returned from the police station with his *sohn* in tow. Recalcitrant and unrepentant, Liam seemed determined to punish everyone around him.

A brittle object shattered. The slam of a door was followed by the thud of heavy footsteps steps descending the stairs outside.

Welcoming the silence, Amity glanced at the curtains spread across the kitchen table. She'd only put up a single valance. The argument next door had completely sucked away the joy she felt in decorating her new apartment. As much as she hated to admit it, it appeared Ethan Zehr and his *youngies* were going to be troublesome neighbors.

Am I making a mistake?

Emotion tightened her throat. A rush of tears blurred her vision. Neck prickling, a spray of goose bumps covered her bare arms. Back home on the ranch, she was part of a large and bustling *familie*. Soon she would be part of, well…nothing.

Aching with loneliness, she abandoned her decorating. The motivation to continue evaporated. Though she'd unlatched the shutters covering the wide bay windows to open the space, emptiness shadowed her. Come evening, almost every business on Main Street closed. The street below was abandoned. As it was Friday, and she'd planned to stay overnight. The shop would be open just half a day tomorrow. After that, she planned to spend her free time arranging her belongings. Now, she wasn't so keen on the idea.

Needing to calm her nerves, she set a kettle atop the stove. She wasn't hungry, but a cup of tea would settle her knotted stomach. Filling a metal ball with a loose-leaf herbal blend, she let it steep before pouring a cup of the steaming brew.

Drink in hand, she carried it to the sofa. Her Bible and study notes were spread out on the coffee table. A basket of knitting sat nearby. Her friend Kitty was expecting a *boppli.* As a gift, she'd begun work on a blanket. Matching booties and a hat would finish the ensemble.

Sipping her tea, she looked around. The walk-up apartment was one of the reasons she was keen to buy in to the building. Perfect for a single person, the floor plan was open, combining a kitchenette with the living room. A bathroom, two small bedrooms and a utility closet large enough to hold a washer and dryer finished the space.

Now, it was almost finished. Walls painted white, she'd chosen a soft shade of sage for the trim. The curtains she'd made were fringed in a darker green, complementing the throw pillows she'd made for the sofa. To set off the floral print, she'd added an area rug. Twin barrel chairs with matching end tables created a cozy nook to sit and visit. The cedar chest doubling as a seat in front of the large bay window offered additional storage. Tasteful knickknacks, such as her grandmother's notions box and a pair of antique lamps, filled bare spaces atop the tables. The highlight of the room was the gas-powered fireplace that replicated the coziness of a wood-burning hearth.

She took a deep breath, and then another. Picking up her

Bible, she returned to the passage she'd marked in Proverbs. *She considereth a field, and buyeth it: with the fruit of her hands she planteth a vineyard.*

Following the Biblical principle, she'd done exactly that. Overruling her grandson's desire to sell for a tidy profit, Charlotte Dekker had let her purchase the property at a price lower than the market value. The old lady's generosity was an act of encouragement toward a fellow businesswoman.

Normally, an Amish woman lived with her *familie* until the day she wed. But the chance to marry had always eluded her. For better or worse, she would have to support herself. There was no shame in it, either. Shopkeeping was a respectable vocation for a single Amish female. And the home she'd made for herself was clean, neat and decent. She was truly blessed.

Bowing her head, Amity immersed herself in her studies. The changes in her life weren't going to be easy, but they were manageable. *Gott's* holy words were a balm, calming and refreshing her battered spirit.

Three hard thuds on her front door made her raise her eyes. The interruption was unexpected.

After slipping a marker between the pages, she crossed to the door and cracked it open. Charity stood outside.

"*Poppi* sent me over to apologize for the noise." Clutching a platter wrapped in foil, she thrust it out. "If you'd care to have it, he sent cold cuts, cheese and bread for your supper."

"How lovely." Stepping back, Amity gestured toward the counter. "Come in, please. You can set that just there. I'm afraid I've got the table cluttered with my sewing."

Charity scurried in, doing as instructed. "Oh, my. You've done so much since I last saw it." Her curious gaze probed every inch.

Amity shut the door, leaving it unbolted. "Do you like it?"

"*Ja.* I do. I wish *Datt* would do more to make ours look better."

"Men don't usually think about things like that." Folding the curtains, she moved them off the table. "It's up to us women to make a *haus* a home."

The girl's expression darkened. "It doesn't feel much like home since we moved here. All *Datt* and Liam do is fight. *Poppi* tries to keep the peace, but it isn't working." Sadness laced her voice.

Amity gave the *youngie* a long look. Though she was only a child, dark circles rimmed her eyes. Worry and stress had formed lines around the edges of her mouth. The plain gray *kapp* and frock she wore gave her the look of a prisoner serving time.

The poor girl has no happiness, no joy.

As far as she knew, the only socialization Charity got was working in the *kaffeeshop*. Even then, the labor was no fun. The child needed a chance to spend time with others her age, but she doubted Ethan noticed his youngest. He was busy with an unruly teenager. After Sheriff Miller's arrival, Ethan sent Charity home. Pale and angry, he'd accompanied the sheriff downtown.

"I know settling in a new place is hard, and you've not had a chance to make new friends," she said. "But school will start soon and that will change, I know. Until then, there are things you can do for fun."

"Like what?"

"Do you have any hobbies?" She gestured toward her basket of yarn. "Knitting perhaps?"

Charity nodded. "I used to do embroidery. But I had to leave some of my things when we moved. *Datt* said I could get more, but I think he forgot. All he does is try to make Liam mind. He bought him the bike, but Liam doesn't like it." Expression turning envious, she added, "He wants an electric scooter."

Amity recalled the bicycle in question. Instead of a slick ten-speed or something a teen *boi* would find more fashionable, Ethan had invested in a cargo-style bicycle. Made for carrying groceries and other bulky items, the bikes were popular among Amish youths, who often chose them over a horse and buggy for short-distance travel. Unhappy with the choice, Liam often sped recklessly up and down the sidewalks. One time he'd been going so fast he'd almost sent one of her shopgirls flying. Barely able to catch herself, Sophie had lost her grip on her basket. The jars of fresh honey she carried shattered. After angrily catching up with Liam, Sophie demanded the *boi* pay for the damaged items. Laughing, Liam had refused.

"Seems like your *bruder* is ungrateful."

Charity rolled her eyes. "*Ach*, that he is." Wincing, she added, "He pinches me if I say anything, so I don't. I just do my best to stay away from him. I stay in my room, mostly. But there's nothing much to do but read and write stories."

Amity tucked away the tidbit. How Ethan chose to handle his *familie* was his business. Still, she felt he should be told about the abuse Liam was leveraging against his younger sibling. In her mind, bullying wasn't acceptable on any level. When she got a chance, she intended to have a word with him. Ethan might not like hearing it, but he would know about it.

As she didn't feel it was fair Liam had gotten an expensive item and Charity had gotten nothing, she felt compelled to offer the girl something to help ease her boredom.

"I have an embroidery frame and some nice linen if you'd care to have it," she said, making up her mind to extend the hand of friendship to the youngster. "I also have plenty of thread, and it needs to be used before it goes bad."

Charity's expression brightened. "Oh, I would. Very much. *Danke.*"

"Maybe you'd like to join my sewing group, too." Now that her apartment was almost done, she'd planned to invite her friends over. It wouldn't hurt to include Charity. Amish women embraced all sorts of hobbies. Spending time with a needle and thread was a favored activity in the evening after the day's work was done.

The girl's grin widened. "Could I?"

"You'd be most welcome."

"I'd have to ask *Datt.*"

"I'll be glad to speak to him."

"Could you do it now?"

Amity hesitated. After arguing with Liam, Ethan might not be approachable. But Charity's pleading look changed her mind. She'd extended the invitation. It was only fair to follow through.

"Of course."

After checking her *kapp* in a decorative mirror near the door, she opened the door and stepped outside. Side by side, the two apartments shared a common balcony that had an awning. Spiral stairs bracketing each side led to the alley below. Built during a time when it was common for proprietors to live above their shops, the design was quirky but appealing. Across the alley, grassy land hosting a copse of hearty trees served as a rest area and park for the Main Street proprietors and their customers. Covered benches and picnic-style tables offered a place to sit and enjoy a quiet moment.

Ethan was outside, standing near the foot of the stairs.

Waving to catch his attention, Amity hurried down to ground level. Charity followed at her heels. As she stepped onto the pavement, she caught sight of Liam's bike. Usually, the teenager parked it in a niche beneath one of the staircases, secured with a chain and padlock. Now, it was lying in a heap, handlebars twisted and tires flattened. Charity, too, saw the damage.

"What happened?"

Ethan barely glanced up. "Your *bruder* smashed it."

Charity burst into tears. "It wasn't right of him to tear it up."

Bending, Ethan straightened the bike. "It can be fixed," he said, propping in its place. "I'll take it to be repaired when I have a moment." Looking at his daughter, he instructed, "Go check on *Poppi*. Make sure he's taken his pills. I've no doubt Liam's antics got his blood pressure up."

Charity sniffled. "*Ja*, I will."

Amity watched her go. Once again, Charity had been overshadowed by her *bruder*.

Looking from her to the bike, Ethan cleared his throat. Dismay and embarrassment creased his expression. "I apologize. I am sorry you had to hear the shouting."

"The *boi's* out of control," she blurted, unwilling to mince words.

"I know." Despair flared in Ethan's gaze. "Sheriff Miller warned me about those *Englisch bois* he's hanging out with." He lifted his hat and ran a hand through his thick hair before putting it back in its place. "But I don't know how to keep Liam away from them."

Amity's attention shifted back to the damaged bike. Anyone with two eyes could see Liam was treading a dangerous path. Close to becoming a delinquent, the teenager needed a job that would keep him busy from sunup to sundown. The Amish believed in taking a firm hand with their *youngies*. Hard, physical labor was guaranteed to tame a young man's youthful energy.

"I know a place Liam can go to work. He may not like it, but it will straighten him out."

Chapter Four

His gaze sweeping the vast Texas vista, Ethan took in the impressive view. The ranch was huge. Across the gravel drive, a sprawling barn was large enough to stable a dozen horses. Pens teemed with livestock—milk cows, goats, chickens and rabbits, plus a scattering of feral barn cats. Cowhands dressed in shirts, jeans and boots were hard at work. Some rode on horseback with cow dogs trotting behind. Others drove battered old work trucks loaded with hay and other supplies. Across the drive, a ring of sturdy trees bracketed a two-story *haus*. Thick grass covered the lawn. Flower and vegetable gardens were neatly kept. A bunkhouse and other utility buildings occupied other parts of the acreage. Spread as far as the eye could see, a large herd of cattle roamed the gently sloping landscape.

Praise the Lord. This might be the answer I've needed.

"What do you think?" Amity asked.

Ethan unbuckled his seat belt, then opened the door and slid out. "I'm not sure I have the words."

Amity followed him. "It's a lot bigger than people expect."

"All this belongs to your *familie*?"

"*Ja.* My great-grandfather settled here in the thirties. He was part of the group that broke off from the Casselman River congregation. We come from the Old Order, but we're not as strict nowadays. But we are still bound by the desire to live in a way that pleases *Gott*."

Ethan felt a twinge of guilt. Despite the trouble he'd given her, Amity met his every complaint with quiet patience. She'd not once raised her voice or pointed a finger back at him. By all appearances, she was a woman of deep faith. She was also a kind one. Seeing a *youngie* in trouble, she'd offered a helping hand.

"I've begun to understand that." A longing to make things right filled him. "I regret the grief I gave you. I acted like a ridiculous fool."

"I know you had concerns," she said, flagging her hands in good-natured dismissal. "I'm glad you've found some ease."

"With you, *ja*. With my *sohn*… Not so much." Normally, the *kaffeeshop* was open half a day on Saturdays. Determined to find a solution for Liam, he'd closed the café and hired a driver and van for the afternoon.

Amity cocked her head. "I knew a *boi* like Liam. One who lost his *familie* in a buggy accident. He was angry and difficult, too. My *daadi* took him in and put him to work. He grew into a fine man."

"Oh? Where is he now?"

A merry chuckle tinkled out. "He married my *schwester* and they have three *youngies*. If anyone can help set Liam straight, Levi will."

"I look forward to meeting him."

Amity pointed to a nearby corral. Two men dressed in Plain clothing were inside. Mounted on horses, one of the riders circled an ornery calf. "Come. Levi and Seth are there now."

"Sounds *gut*." Nodding, Ethan turned back to the van. Liam, Charity and *Daed* all sat inside. "Remember, we are guests," he said, motioning for them to follow.

Charity clambered out first. "Look at all the animals!"

Daed followed, grinning broadly. "Now this is real country living," he enthused, spreading his arms wide and taking a breath of air. "It's nice to be back in the open."

Liam refused to budge. "I'm not getting out."

Ethan gave his *sohn* a narrow look. Accompanying Sheriff Miller to the county jail to bail out Liam was an embarrassment he doubted he'd ever get over. As a minor, Liam had been released back into his custody, pending an appearance before the municipal court judge. A warning from the lawman included keeping Liam away from his ne'er-do-well friends.

"I've no more tolerance for your behavior," he said, adding an edge to his tone.

Liam poked out his bottom lip. "So?"

Ethan mentally gritted his teeth. Between getting arrested and damaging his bike, Liam had gone far enough. The teen's disruptive behavior was inexcusable. Sheriff Miller had mentioned there was a state facility for *youngies* who were out of control. But the last thing Ethan wanted to do was send his *sohn* into the secular *Englisch* juvenile system. His dearest wish was to keep Liam in the faith—lead him back to *Gott* and the Amish community.

"You'll be going back to the sheriff," he warned. "I'm sure he will be glad to keep you in jail until you see the judge."

Liam's face paled. He reluctantly exited the van. "Don't expect me to like it." The tremble in his voice betrayed his fear. He'd tried to play it tough, but the act wasn't fooling anyone. He was scared. Cuffed and booked, he'd gotten a taste of what it felt like to be on the wrong side of the law. Dark circles beneath his eyes revealed he'd spent a sleepless night.

Ethan dismissed the driver. Promising to return before sunset, the man departed.

"Come," Amity said, and made a motion for everyone to follow. "You can meet some of my *familie*."

Everyone except Liam fell into step. Chattering and pointing, Charity enthused over the rabbits in the pen. They were all so cute, she said, hinting she'd like a bunny for a pet.

Daed grinned broadly, pointing into the distance. "We should look at land out this way."

Ethan gave each half an ear. "Might be something to think about," was his reply to both.

Liam dragged his feet. "I don't like the country anymore," he declared. "All I smell is manure. This place stinks."

Ethan let the remark pass.

Amity did not. "After a day's work, you'll smell just like them."

"You think that's going to happen?" Liam snorted. "Not in a million years."

"Don't be so quick to say no," *Daed* said. "Fresh air and sunshine can do wonders for a man's spirit."

"My spirit says *nein*," Liam grumbled, kicking at the ground.

Charity waggled a finger at her *bruder*. "*Gott* has words for the likes of you. 'Let him that stole steal no more, but rather let him labor, working with his hands.'"

A flush crept into Liam's face. Blanching, he dropped his gaze and hung his head. "You don't have to rub it in. I know I did wrong." Bravado crumbling, he sniffled. He dug the heels of his hands into his eyes. The repercussions were sinking in.

Ethan gave his youngest a look. "*Gott* also says to be merciful. Liam's been called out, and he'll have to deal with the consequences."

Charity's expression dimmed. "I didn't mean to tease."

"I know. It's not our place to judge, but to help."

"Amen," *Daed* murmured. "Wise words, indeed."

Reaching the corral, they stood outside the perimeter. Inside, two men sat on horses. Both were tanned, blond and dressed in Plain clothing. Beneath a battered straw hat, the older man was bearded. The other was not. Across the way, a second older *Englisch* man with a pipe clenched between his teeth leaned into the fence to watch.

The younger rider held a rope in his hand. Spurring his horse into motion, he expertly lassoed one of the calves set loose in the arena. The animal bucked hard, fighting captivity. After sliding off his mount, the rider tackled the calf. He knocked it down, then bound all four legs with expert precision.

The onlookers clapped.

The bearded man checked his watch. "Twelve seconds, Seth. A little slow today."

Freeing the calf, the *youngie* grinned as he gathered his rope. "I'll whittle it down by the time the rodeo comes to town."

The older men laughed. "Don't get too full of yourself," one said.

Amity waved to catch their attention. "Levi! Seth! We have company!"

Leaving their horses behind, the two walked over.

"My name's Levi Wyse. This is Seth, my oldest," one of the men greeted.

Ethan reciprocated, introducing himself. "My *vater*, Wayne. And my *tochter*, Charity."

Levi's gaze drifted toward Liam. "This must be your oldest."

"*Ja.* Liam. Amity said you might have work for him."

Levi eyed the teen from head to foot. "How old are you, *boi*?"

"Fifteen," Liam mumbled, refusing to make eye contact.

"Ever work cattle?"

"Nein."

"We had cattle on our farm," Ethan added helpfully. "But nothing like this."

"These ain't just cows." Removing his hat, Seth wiped the perspiration off his brow with the back of his hand. Gangly but muscular, he stood near a grown man's height. "They're Longhorns. They're ornery and they have a temper. And if you ain't careful, they'll jab you with those horns."

Liam angled his chin. "I'm not scared. I think I could handle one just as *gut* as you."

Seth set his hands on his hips. "Only the tough ones get by out here."

Liam's cocky attitude reared its head. "I can do anything you can. Maybe even better."

The teenagers stared each other down, unsure if they should be rivals or friends.

Stepping between the tense youths, Levi pointed toward the corral. "Instead of arguing the matter, get out there and show us what you can do."

Liam's gaze sparked as he eyed the horses. "Yes!"

The two young men raced to the corral. Seth hefted himself onto his horse with expert ease. Liam took Levi's horse. Within minutes, they were galloping around. Liam's grin was a mile wide as he circled the corral. Challenged by a peer, he was out to prove he could give as good as he got.

Seth signaled to the *Englischer* smoking his pipe. "Open up, Ezra! We're heading out to rile a few cows."

Ezra complied. Gates thrown wide, the horses dashed with the freedom to run without restriction.

Watching them go, Ethan felt relief well up. Liam had ridden since he was old enough to walk. Having no place to stable horses while living in town, they'd had to leave the animals behind.

Charity clapped he hands. "Look at them go!"

"Been a while since he's looked that happy," *Daed* said. "I like seeing him smile again."

Ethan agreed. He turned to Levi. "Think you can use him?"

"I'm sure I can find something for him to do," Levi replied, readjusting his hat to cut the angle of the sun.

"I'll be honest and tell you Liam was arrested for stealing. Those *Englisch bois* he hangs around with egged him on."

Levi rolled his eyes. "The *Englisch* world can be trouble when our *youngies* start their *rumspringa*."

"Liam's only fifteen but he's champing at the bit to live in their world. Can't say that's what I want for either of my *kinder*."

"I agree. I spent ten years in the *Englisch* world. I know how it is."

Ethan's eyebrows rose. "Really?"

A grin crinkled the corners of Levi's eyes. "*Ja*. Didn't like what I saw, either."

"Then you understand why I want Liam away from those hooligans?"

"I do. And I guarantee Liam will be so busy he won't have time to find any trouble. We work from sunup to sundown, six days a week. And since he'll be working like a man, he'll be paid like a man." Levi stuck out his hand. "Fair enough?"

Ethan accepted. "Fair enough."

The heavy clang of a bell filled the air. Leaving their work behind, the hired hands began to drift in for the afternoon meal.

"It's time for lunch, so we'll hammer out the details later,"

Levi announced. "I hope you're all hungry. My *ehefrau* puts out quite a spread."

Daed grinned and patted his stomach. "I could eat a bite or three," he boomed in his hearty way.

"If it's no trouble," Ethan added, giving his *daed* a sharp look.

Amity shook her head. "*Ach*, it's no trouble at all. The more, the merrier."

"We follow *Gott's* word and welcome all," Levi added. "When you are here, you are *familie*."

Gratitude tightened Ethan's throat. He liked these people. A lot. "*Danke* for inviting us."

Now that he'd learned his lesson, he looked forward to getting to know more about them and their way of life.

"Now that I've met Ethan, he isn't as bad as I imagined," Rebecca said. "I'd pictured quite an imposing man."

Hands plunged in soapy water, Gail nodded. "I think he's nice." Washing each dish carefully, she handed one over. "I like him."

Towel in hand, Amity dried the plates and cups. "He wasn't so friendly when I first met him," she said, placing each dish in its place with care. "But he had a change of heart. He's apologized several times for his complaints."

All in all, the meal had gone well. Everyone seemed to enjoy themselves. Eating with a hearty appetite, Wayne Zehr had declared it to be the best food he'd ever eaten. The old man said Gail cooked like his dear *ehefrau*, Letha. Ethan had agreed, saying the *melassich riwwelboi,* or shoofly pie as it was called, tasted exactly the way his *mamm* made it.

With lunch over, the men and the *youngies* were sent outside to allow the women a chance to clean up. Levi had taken Sammy in hand, giving Gail a much-needed break. Firmly planted on the living room sofa, Florene kept half an eye on baby Jessica. Safely ensconced in her bassinet, the *boppli* dozed with contentment.

Rebecca wiped down the table with a damp rag. "I'd prayed the Lord would soften his thoughts on the matter."

"It's easy to understand why he was concerned. The brethren he comes from are much stricter than ours. Honestly, I might have been inclined to make the same complaints if I stood in his place."

"It's a concern we should all have, strict or not. The internet opens the door to temptation," Gail said. "It's nothing I want my *youngies* exposed to."

Tossing her rag into a hamper, Rebecca released a long sigh. "Unfortunately, we have to find a way to deal with the technology in our community now. It's here to stay. And, as the bishop said, it's up to each individual to decide how much or how little they care to use it."

Dishes done, Gail let the water drain out of the basin. "I don't care to use it at all. Even a cell phone is too much for me. Levi likes having one, though I can't say I'm sorry our coverage is hit-and-miss out here."

"We need better reception in these parts," Rebecca countered. "Caleb has to have a phone for his work. I do want him to be safe when he's traveling."

Amity gave each a long look. On one hand, she agreed with Gail. On the other, she took Rebecca's side. Technology—a computer, the internet and phones—had pros and cons. It was a fine balancing act, preserving the traditions of the past while embracing the future.

"The Lord warns that people are destroyed by their lack of knowledge. But I think these things are like rattlesnakes. Dangerous if prodded."

"Oh, posh!" Florene said to disagree. "I use my phone

all the time. It hasn't jumped up and bitten me yet." As the youngest, she was more open to the *Englisch* and their technology. She'd recently dropped a few hints that she planned to leave the community.

"Don't be so sure about that," Gail warned. "You're too tied up in that thing."

Florene shrugged. "So? I like the dating apps. It's the way to meet people now."

Amity winced over her sister's remarks. Now going on twenty-one, Florene's *rumspringa* was winding to a close. Traditionally, she should have chosen her intended, and started preparing for her baptism and marriage to a Plain man. No one was happy she continued to look outside the Amish community for companionship.

"I wouldn't think that would be safe," Rebecca cautioned. "Meeting a stranger you met online."

"How is it any different from what Amity does? She advertises in the personals section of *Thrifty Living.* She's looking for a man."

"The ad is for a pen pal," Amity squeaked, horrified by the way Florene made it sound.

"Having a correspondent is different," Rebecca said.

"How?"

"For one, it's anonymous. They don't know who you are. At least, not right away. When someone responds, you can decide to answer them. Or not. And their words are on paper, giving you a chance to get to know them through their writing." Done with her explanation, Rebecca set her hands on her slender waist. A former schoolteacher, she knew how to back up her words with a formidable scowl to silence the naysayers.

Rolling her eyes, Florene turned her smartphone. "So how is that any different from online dating? I can look at a profile and see if it's someone I want to talk to. Aren't you taking a chance the person you're corresponding with isn't who they say they are? Anyone who reads the paper could answer your ad. And you wouldn't know who they were until you met face-to-face. Right?"

Gail glowered at the offending cell phone. "I suppose it is somewhat the same," she allowed. As the oldest, she did her best to keep the peace when squabbles broke out.

Florene's expression turned smug. "Told you. It's just another way to reach out to people. I prefer to do it digitally, is all."

A bit upset that she hadn't quite won the argument, Rebecca sniffed with disdain. "Well, Miss Know It All, is there someone online you intend to see in person?"

"That's for me to know and you to find out." A mysterious smile lifted the edges of Florene's mouth. She looked to Amity. "You?"

Amity was reluctant to reply. As hard as she tried, she simply could not seem to make a lasting connection with any man. "Honestly, I don't know," she said, preferring to keep her answer vague. "I've been so busy with the store and moving into town that I haven't had time to check my box." It was kind of, sort of, the truth. She did check. Once a week. Her box was so empty it was beginning to gather dust.

Discouragement choked her into silence. Loneliness gnawed. She felt hollow. Worthless. A rise of tears blurred her vision. Florene knew exactly her Achilles' heel. She'd deliberately pushed her verbal thorn in deep. Unwilling to let Florene make her cry, she tamped down her emotions.

The *boppli* began to fuss, causing Gail to sweep the infant into her arms. "*Ach*, someone's cranky after her nap," she said, soothing Jessica's cries with kisses.

Rebecca gave the pair a fond smile. "I'm sure some playtime will do wonders."

"I'm tired of watching babies." Florene's phone pinged, prompting her to check her messages. "Looks like Kaya will be by later."

Gail's lips tightened into a frown of disapproval. "Going out?"

"Of course. What else would I do on a Saturday? Sit home knitting?" Grinning, she laughed merrily. "No way!" Tossing a wave, she disappeared up the stairs.

Amity sighed. That was exactly what she would probably be doing. Sitting at home. Knitting.

Rebecca offered a quick hug of encouragement. "Don't let Florene bother you."

"It's okay. It's just Florene."

Gail frowned. "That girl has always had a selfish streak. I pray *Gott* will get hold of her."

"No reason to wait on *Gott*." Waggling a finger, Rebecca headed toward the stairs. "I intend to have a word with her now."

Holding Jessica, Gail stepped up to bump Amity with her shoulder. "Don't let Florene dim your day. Come on. It will do you *gut* to get some fresh air."

Walking toward the back door, they exited the kitchen. A sturdy awning shaded the patio, offering a break from direct sunlight. A picnic table, benches and other chairs gave folks a place to sit. A copse of trees circled a quarter of the house, providing a windbreak and additional shade. Rope swings dangled from overhanging branches. An old tractor tire filled with sand invited digging. A treehouse beckoned climbers to come inside.

Seth and Liam sat at the table. With diligent concentration, they worked on a puzzle Seth had recently acquired.

Haunting a tangle of shrubbery, Charity attempted to coax a litter of kittens out of hiding. Feral and unkempt, the tiny cats hissed and spit. Walking on wobbly legs, one of the smaller felines dared to sniff the tips of her fingers.

Latching on to Ethan's *daed*, Sammy had persuaded the old man to play. Mixing soap and water, Wayne showed him how to create bubbles. Sammy squealed with delight as he popped them. "More, *Poppi*!" he cried, clapping happily. Wayne obliged, sending a flurry of iridescent orbs into the air. Sammy giggled and chased them.

Levi and Ethan were engaged in animated conversation. Close to the same age, the men laughed like old friends.

"Mind if we join you?" Gail asked.

"Not at all." Levi rose, giving her his chair.

"Feel kind of bad visiting while you ladies do all the work." Ethan cranked to his feet and made a motion for Amity to sit.

Preferring to stand, she declined. "I'm fine. *Danke*."

Gail sat, settling Jessica in her lap. The toddler wiggled and fussed to be set free. "No room for men in my kitchen. And no guest of mine is expected to wash dishes."

"Ethan was asking about land for sale," Levi explained, bringing them in on the conversation. "He's thinking about buying a piece of property."

Amity perked up. She knew just the place. "I was talking to Jenna Klatch last week. She mentioned Giles wanted to sell their farm."

Levi snapped his fingers. "Believe I heard the same thing. Their place would be worth considering. Big *haus*, a barn, a place to keep livestock."

"Their land borders the Stetler orchards," Gail added. "Alva Stetler grows some fine apples and peaches. Pecans, too. Her produce makes the best pies."

Ethan cocked his head. "I'd be interested. Have they set a price?"

"Not sure," Amity said.

Levi looked between the two. "You could always ride out and ask."

"I wouldn't want to show up uninvited."

"Guess you haven't gotten used to hospitality in these parts," Gail laughed. "Living far from town, we love it when folks come by. Jenna always has a kettle on the stove. Most of us do."

"Why they'd be offended if you didn't." Levi added a wink. "And don't say no to Jenna's *butterkuchen*. She always cuts a thick slice for company."

"If you wouldn't mind my *youngies* and *daed* staying here, I'd like to look. Maybe speak to the man."

Gail gave Jessica a bounce on her knee to quiet her wriggling *youngie*. "They're having a fine time. Why bother them?"

"I'll have one of the hands hitch up the wagon and Amity can take you over," Levi volunteered. "That will give you a chance to get out and see some of the countryside."

Unexpectedly thrust into the role of tour guide, Amity's pulse kicked up. "I suppose we could…" Dismay rippled through her the moment the agreement left her mouth.

What is Levi thinking? Sending me to spend time alone… with Ethan Zehr…

Chapter Five

Reins in hand, Levi guided the wagon to the front of the barn. The mare whinnied, ready for a day out. "Here you go."

Hands on his hips, Ethan gave an approving glance. "I sure miss having horses. Had to sell them when we moved. When we get a place, a horse and buggy will be the first thing I'll buy."

"I know where you can pick up some *gut* workhorses," Levi said. "Gil Kestler brings down wild mustangs from New Mexico. He breaks them into fine dray animals." He patted the hearty mare on the neck. "Got this one and a few others from him."

"I'll keep that in mind."

"They're still the best way to travel if you ask me," Levi said behind a wide grin.

Amity didn't quite agree. Levi had picked the slowest mare in the stable. The journey would take twice as long.

"We should get going," she prompted.

Ethan grinned. "Ready when you are."

Levi pulled the hand brake to keep the wagon in place, then looped the reins around it. "Enjoy the ride." Giving a wave, he ambled off to speak to a couple of cowhands.

Mumbling under her breath at the inconvenience, Amity caught a handful of her skirt and attempted to climb up into the buckboard. Her foot missed the lower step. Losing her grip, she pitched backward. The hard ground loomed below.

"Oh…!"

Strong hands blocked her fall. "Have a care," Ethan breathed, setting her on her feet.

Flustered, Amity stumbled away. Her pulse quickened, sending a rush of adrenaline through her veins. "I'm so clumsy."

"Forgive me for forgetting my manners. A man should always offer a hand."

She pulled in a breath to steady her trembling legs. His touch had completely discombobulated her, and she didn't understand why. "It was entirely my fault. I should have been paying attention to what I was doing."

"Would you rather not go?"

Amity remembered his anticipation when they'd discussed the property, and again when the wagon rolled out. Working in a shop, he probably looked forward to spending time outside on his days off.

"Nein," she said, shaking her head. "It will be nice to get out and enjoy this fine weather we're having."

"I agree." Ethan held out his hand. "May I?"

Amity hesitated before sliding her hand into his. *"Danke."* His grip was sure and firm as he hoisted her onto the wooden seat. Smoothing her skirt across her lap, she tucked it beneath her legs. Black granny-style boots, flat-heeled and laced high, concealed her ankles. Every other inch of bare skin was covered except for her arms, neck and face. Because the wagon was an open one, there would be no need for a male member of her *familie* to ride along as a chaperone. They weren't on any sort of walkabout, and it wasn't a courting buggy. She folded her hands in her lap, determined to keep a decent distance. No reason to give onlookers any ideas.

Circling the front of the mare, Ethan settled on the driver's side. "Shall we go?" Without waiting for a reply, he claimed the reins. Clucking his tongue, he expertly flicked one of the leather strips against the horse's rump. Releasing a hearty chuff, the horse lunged forward into a slow walk. The wagon rolled, making a familiar creaking sound.

Levi waved them off. "Have a nice drive!" The cowhands he stood with also raised their hands in acknowledgment.

"We'll be back," Ethan called as he followed the drive circling between the house and the barn. Cradling the kitten she'd captured, Charity watched from the perimeter of the backyard. Gail, too, called out something in *Deitsch*, but her words were unintelligible as they passed.

Keeping the horse at a steady pace, Ethan followed the long stretch of gravel road leading to the highway. Reaching the end, he pulled to a halt. Save for a stop sign and a marker on a steel pole that read CR 22 there were no other nearby signs to indicate location or what might come next.

He looked right and then left. "I didn't realize how remote it is. I bet it's easy to get lost out here."

"*Ja.* Some folks can't find their way here, even with a GPS. Ours is thankfully marked. It's called Rabbit Road because of all the wild hares. Everyone knows it because we've been here so long."

Ethan pushed back his straw hat. Loose curls brushed his strong brow. "I believe it is important for people to have roots, to belong to the land." Offering a brief smile, his expression softened with longing. "Being out here, you understand what it means when *Gott* said we should abide in peaceful habitation."

Amity visually tracked his gaze. The endless sloping

plains stretched as far as the eye could see. Thick wild grass and other flora nourished the livestock roaming the wide-open spaces. Born and raised on the homestead founded by her *urgrobvater*, her pending move weighed on her heart. She would miss her *familie* and the peace of the rural countryside. Emotion squeezed her throat. An apartment in town would never be her true home. But the decision was made, and she'd stick with it.

"Turn left," she instructed. "Then turn right at the clump of trees about five miles down. That road will get us to the Klatch farm."

Amusement lifted one corner of his mouth. "That's it? Turn at the trees?"

"That's the way we give directions. 'Down yonder,' 'a while away,' and 'over thereabout' are all valid directions. These farm roads go here, there and everywhere. It's confusing, but most lead to a homestead or back into town."

His nostrils flared with amusement. "Guess I'll have to learn to speak Texan if I plan to stay around these parts."

Giving the horse a tap with the reins, Ethan turned the wagon onto the long stretch of highway. The mare bore her burden with patience, plodding along. The wheels clattered. Traveling on a public highway, the wagon was outfitted with safety features that would make it more visible to *Englisch* drivers. Eighteen-wheelers and other large trucks often presented a hazard to slower vehicles.

Amity fanned a hand in front of her face, wishing she'd remembered to grab an umbrella to cut the glare. The wagon was an open one, leaving them exposed to the elements. Thankfully, a flurry of clouds driven by a light breeze pushed back summer's intense heat.

Shading her eyes, she surveyed the open countryside. She'd gotten used to the convenience of riding in a gas-powered vehicle. It was easy to forget how pleasant and re-laxing it was to ride slower, less hurriedly. The sound of the horse's hooves clomping on the ground was soothing and rhythmic. Tipping back her head, she closed her eyes. Sun-shine warmed her skin. She felt peaceful. Calm. She was glad she'd agreed to come.

Finding the turn she'd indicated, Ethan followed it. As Levi had warned, the road wasn't the smoothest to travel. Deep ruts caused them to brush shoulders more than once.

Clutching the seat, Amity pulled herself straight. "Sorry," she mumbled. The road was rougher than she remembered. But the mare did her job, pulling the wagon over the craggy patches. Another mile disappeared, and then another. The end of the lane revealed a rambling home. A barn and other small buildings sat nearby, as did pens for keeping the ani-mals. Nothing was new and had sat in place for at least half a century.

A fence at the boundary of the property kept trespass-ers at bay. Roused from his afternoon nap in a shady spot, a large shepherd jumped to his feet. Rushing forward, the dog barked a warning.

Ethan stopped the wagon outside the gate. "Looks like we made it." After pulling the hand brake and securing the reins, he jumped down to the ground. Interest sparked in his gaze. "You're sure they're planning to sell?" he asked, walking the perimeter.

"Jenna told me so herself." Taking care not to snag her skirt, she climbed down off the high seat. This time she managed to keep her footing and not make a fool of herself.

"Any reason why?"

"It's not my story to tell. If they care to say, then they will."

"Fair enough."

Lifting a hand to shield her eyes, Amity looked around. Time had taken its toll. Weathered and faded, the old barn screamed out for a fresh whitewashing. The roof on the *haus* had sacrificed more than a few shingles to the intense spring winds that often blasted the landscape. The old farm wasn't in bad shape, but it would be if maintenance wasn't applied within a reasonable amount of time. "I remember how nice it was when I was a girl. It's sad to see it so run-down."

Ethan's expression grew shadowed. "As much as we don't like it everything grows old and withers away. All we can do is accept it and rely on the word of *Gott* to guide us through." Gaze connecting with hers, his lips twitched into a tentative smile. "Other things might change in our lives, but the Lord does not."

Amity looked at him with admiration. "Amen," she murmured.

The dog's noisy barking prompted a response. The front door opened. An elderly man dressed in trousers, a shirt, suspenders and black boots stepped onto the porch. Tall but shockingly thin, he leaned on a cane. "Hush, Rupert!" he scolded, waggling a finger at the hound. He limped down the stairs, and then closed the distance between the house and the fence. Face lined, his skin was leathery from years spent toiling under the unforgiving sun. "Who's there?"

Shocked by her neighbor's decline, Amity forced a smile. Busy with her pursuits, she hadn't bothered to come by in at least a year. Maybe even longer. A big bear of a man, there was a time when Giles Klatch could pick up a heifer and throw it over his shoulders with ease. Now in his eighties, he could barely get around.

"It's me, Giles. Amity," she called over the fence. "Jenna said the farm was going up for sale. I've bought someone who wants to speak to you about it."

"Happy to." Giles Klatch waved a gnarled hand toward the entrance. "Tell your young fella to unlatch the gate and bring your wagon in."

"Would you care for another slice?" Spatula in hand, Jenna Klatch stood prepared to serve more of her vanilla Bundt cake. Puttering around her kitchen, her lively gaze sparkled with good humor.

Swallowing his last bite, Ethan declined. "One slice is about all I can handle," he said, laying his fork across his empty plate. Drizzled with homemade icing, the cake was rich and delicious. He'd enjoyed every bite.

"Amity?" Jenna asked.

Grinning through a groan, Amity shook her head. "No thank you, I'm stuffed."

Finishing his dessert, Giles Klatch showed snaggly teeth. "Plenty more if you change your mind."

"There's too much here for me and Giles," Jenna added. "I'll wrap some for you to take home."

"That would be lovely."

Tuning out the chatter between the women, Ethan reached for his mug. His tea—served black, hot and sweet—was strong enough to grow hair on rocks. It wasn't to his taste. But it had been served in kindness. He would drink it without complaint and insist he'd enjoyed every sip.

Forcing himself to swallow, he looked around. The Klatches' home was simple but cozy. Most everything was handmade, crafted with care and built to last. It had a rambling living arrangement, blending the kitchen and living room into one large space. To divide the two and provide heat to both, the woodburning stove had been bricked into the foundation wall. To support its weight, the floor was made of square paving stones. The design was clever and practical. To make things more attractive, thick rugs were spread throughout. Simple white curtains covered the windows. True, the wallpaper was faded, and a couple of the floorboards squeaked, but the flaws could be repaired.

It was a Plain home. Nothing fancy.

"You're looking for a piece of land?" Giles gave a prod with the tip of his cane, intending to get the conversation going between the menfolk.

Ethan lowered his cup. "I am."

"The word's out we're selling. But I'd have to say I don't like the folks who've inquired."

"Why not?"

"Englischers." Frowning, Giles made a spitting sound. "So cute, they say. So charming. Then they talk about the changes they'll want to make."

Sensing Giles's distress, Jenna limped up. More mobile than her elderly spouse, it was obvious the hard stone floor caused her pain. Bent with arthritis, each step revealed her discomfort. "Pay them no mind," she soothed. "It's just talk."

Displeasure deepening, the old man went on. "I'd not sell to a single one, no matter how much money they have in hand." His mouth turned to a firm pucker of disapproval. "I'd rather see it all go to ruin."

"I'd hate to see that happen," Ethan said. "It's a fine piece of property to raise a *familie* on."

"Aye," Giles said. "My *daadi* was born here, and so was I. Married Jenna and raised our *youngies* here. I'd intended for my *sohn* to do the same." Voice cracking with agony, he pressed his lips flat. Lines of despair etched his eyes and mouth.

"We lost Malachi thirty years ago," Jenna Klatch said, taking up the story. "A rattlesnake spooked his horse, and he was thrown." Her rheumy eyes grew moist with memory. "He didn't survive."

"He was our only *youngie*," Giles said sadly. "*Gott* didn't see fit to bless us with more. We'd hoped when he married Grace that the *haus* would be filled with *kinder* again."

Sympathy prodded. "Have you no *enkelkinder*?"

"Aye. One. But he's gone, too. His *mamm* took him away."

"Grace left Burr Oak about a year after Malachi passed." Trembling, Jenna wiped the tears from her eyes. "Said it hurt too much to stay. She moved to Maine. The community there is small but growing. The bishop was welcoming to any who'd come. Last we heard, she'd remarried. Never heard from her again. And Enoch was too small to remember us. Doubt we'll ever see him again."

Ethan's heart thudded in his chest. The elderly couple's narrative was heart-wrenching.

Knowing the facts, he couldn't entirely blame Grace Klatch for wanting to move away. He understood the young widow's agony more than he cared to admit.

Needing a breath of air to clear his head, he nodded toward the door. "Would you mind if I took a walk around?"

"Not at all," Giles said. "I wouldn't expect a man to make any sort of an offer without seeing what he'd get first." His grip tightened on the head of his cane. He attempted to push himself to his feet. He only made it halfway. Legs shaking beneath his weight, he sat back down.

"Can't do it. Lost my strength since the diabetes set in." Embarrassment created his face. "Don't know what happened. One day I turned around and found I'd got old."

Ethan nodded in sympathy. His *daed* struggled with his blood pressure and other small ailments. Doctors had warned him to stay on his medication and to cut down on rich foods. It was hard to do since the Amish were hearty eaters. Most old-fashioned cooks used heaps of butter, lard and rich cream in their recipes.

Jenna fretted, wringing her hands. "We can't stay here. Dr. Sutter told Giles it'd be better if we were in town. We're moving as soon as the farm is sold."

"Where will you go?" Amity asked.

"Rebecca put us in touch with Elva Schrock," Jenna explained. "We'll be renting her old *dawdy haus*. Rebecca won't be taking it after all, so it was still available."

Amity laughed. Before meeting Caleb Sutter, Rebecca had planned to move into town and open a day care for *Englisch kinder*.

"Rebecca will have her hands full enough after she marries. Their new *haus* is close to being finished and they're planning to fill it with *youngies* as soon as they can."

"The doctor has been a blessing. It's hard enough getting Giles into town, so having a physician who comes to us has helped. He said it would make more sense for us to live in town, and I agree."

Sighing heavily, Giles shook his head. "I don't like the idea of leaving the place I was born. But my health isn't *gut* anymore. And when I pass, Jenna would be out here alone. The property would be too much for her to handle."

"Elva said she'd rent to us at a reasonable price," Jenna said, laying a hand on her *ehmann's* shoulder. "Being in town, we'll be able to get out and visit more often. I've missed going to my quilting circle, but it's such trouble to hitch the wagon and go." Anticipation brightened her gaze.

Amity flashed her engaging smile. "I'd say the Lord worked everything out perfectly."

"He always does," Giles finished softly. "And that's why I know *Gott* will bring the right folks to our doorstep."

Ethan pushed his chair back. "Don't trouble yourself to

get up. I can always come back some other time to see the rest of the property."

Jenna Klatch shook her head. "Oh, nonsense. You're here now so you might as well look." She motioned at Amity. "You grew up playing here. Why don't you show him the pond?"

Ethan perked up. "There's a pond?"

Amity grinned. "Oh, *ja*! I'd forgotten about it."

"I'd like to see it."

"Go on," Giles urged. "We'll be here when you get back."

Amity pushed back her chair. "Come on. I'll show you."

Ethan rose, following her outside. Just a hop and a skip beyond the backyard was a wide swatch of uncultivated land. Covering a good half acre, maybe more, a gathering of hearty trees, shrubs, wildflowers and buffalo grass created a picturesque tangle around a small pond. A gathering of irregular paving stones provided a walkway. A moss-covered stone bench nestled beneath the spread of outstretched branches offered a cool place to rest. A nearby windmill provided a steady trickle of fresh water. The peaceful sounds of nature embraced them.

Amity smiled merrily. "The pond's been here long as I can remember. *Mamm* used to bring us when she came to visit," she said, leading him over a gentle slope to the water's edge. "We'd come out here to catch the tadpoles and feed the fish. There are mudbugs, too, but they're not very *gut* for eating."

"Mudbugs?"

"Crawdads," she corrected.

"Ah. Never heard them called that before." A flicker of movement beneath the water caught his eye. Seconds later, a gathering of fish appeared. Large with bulging eyes, most were a golden hue. A few odd ones were white with dapples of orange.

"They've come to eat." She bent, poking at a mushy spot

along the edge of the water. "When I was a kid, we'd dig for worms and catch bugs to feed them. Oh, and there's turtles, too. I had one for a pet when I was about eight."

"I don't know anyone who had a pet turtle."

"Oh, I did." She crinkled her nose most endearingly. "His name was Torby. Can't remember what that was supposed to mean. Anyway, he lived to quite a ripe old age."

"That might be perfect for Charity. She's been begging for a pet."

"I saw she latched on to one of the kittens."

Ethan nodded. He'd noticed the Klatch place also had sleek black cats. Anywhere livestock was kept, mice were bound to infest the hay and grain. Most rural folks wanted the felines to help control the rodent population. He didn't mind cats. Priscilla had kept a striped tabby named Thomas. Like so many other things, the animal was left behind when they left Oklahoma. Charity had bawled for days over the loss.

"They're feral and usually won't let anyone touch them," she continued when he didn't reply. "I'm surprised she was able to catch one."

Rolling his eyes, he shook his head. "Now she'll want to take it home. *Daed* will probably take her side. Then I'll have a fight on my hands."

"Hope not." Her cheerful smile widened. "What do you think?"

Hands on his hips, Ethan turned to survey the *haus* and nearby barn. Most of the fixes would be minor, requiring a little elbow grease and commitment. New shingles and a few coats of paint would go a long way. Stepping on the property was like walking back in time. It was comfortable.

When he'd moved to Texas, he'd hated everything about the state. His view had changed dramatically now that he'd opened his eyes. Putting aside his narrow prejudice of what a proper Amish community should be, he'd found himself welcomed with open arms and warm smiles. Texas folks were naturally friendly people. The Amish Texans were doubly so.

It's a place I believe we could call home.

"I like it. It's got possibilities."

"Giles has it in his mind he'll only sell to Amish."

"I'd be interested to know what he's asking."

"There's only one way to find out." She gave him an encouraging look. "I know he'd like the idea of selling to someone with *youngies*." As she spoke, a look of longing came into her eyes. "If I were married, I'd want it. I'd love to raise my own here."

Surprise lifted his brows. "You plan to have a *familie*?"

"Someday." Her gaze grew wistful. "That's what I'm praying for."

Sensing her sadness, Ethan returned the look. Pulse bumping up a notch, warmth curled through his insides. Lively and humorous, his former nemesis had proven herself an entertaining companion.

The pleasant afternoon was winding down, but he wasn't ready for the day to end. They hadn't even parted but he was already considering a time when he could see her again. Soon, he hoped.

Oddly discombobulated, he shoved his hands in his pockets and stared down at his boots. He felt like a deer, caught in the headlights of a fast-moving vehicle. All these feelings were so new. So unexpected.

Pulling in a breath, he stammered out an answer. "I'll p-pray *Gott* answers us both."

Chapter Six

Nothing feels right...

Cracking open her eyes after a restless night, Amity gazed around the unfamiliar room. The furniture she'd had at the ranch now occupied a new space. Everything was hers, but nothing felt like it belonged.

Throwing aside her blanket, she sat up. The modest room was adorned with handmade quilts and neatly organized household items, reflecting the simplicity of her lifestyle. Curtains were tied back with neat bows. A rag rug added a splash of color. The single narrow window offered little natural illumination. Used to waking up with a wide swath of sunlight filling her bedroom, the muted ambiance was a drastic change.

After church, Levi, Caleb and a few hired hands had delivered the last of her possessions. Anticipating the arrival of another *boppli*, Gail was planning to redecorate the room she'd vacated.

That's the way it was supposed to work. Amish couples welcomed as many *kinder* as *Gott* saw fit to bless them with. And single Amish women were expected to marry and join their *ehmann's* household. As she had no decent prospects, the move was her attempt to embrace the role of a single, modern *fraulein*. One who could earn her living.

After drawing in a breath, she murmured, "This is my home. I will be strong and of *gut* courage. For *Gott* is with me wherever I go." Leaning on faith, she would never be forsaken. She also had the church, her business and many friends.

Emboldened, she pushed herself to her feet. She padded into the bathroom, then washed her face and brushed her teeth before dressing for the day. Breakfast was spare—a cup of cambric tea and bread slathered with homemade butter and peach preserves. The only thing that wasn't missing was the cacophony of an active household. The walls between the two living spaces were thin. A multitude of sounds, heavy footfalls and voices filtered through from the Zehr apartment. The *kaffeeshop* opened early, prompting a flurry of activity at the crack of dawn.

Amity cocked her head, listening to the *familie* get ready for their day. The afternoon she'd spent with Ethan was an enjoyable one. They'd had a fine time visiting Jenna and Giles Klatch. Both were attentive hosts. After Ethan had walked the property, the two men had done some figuring, going back and forth on the numbers. Giles had set his price. Ethan was interested. He'd even gone so far as to inquire about making another visit the following day. He wanted to bring his *daed* and *youngies* out to see the place before making a final decision. Giles had declared it was a fine idea. Exchanging handshakes, the two men had agreed to meet after Sunday services. Troubled with health issues, Giles only left home to attend church. Neighbors took turns picking up the elderly couple, as well as helping with errands and other chores.

Sunday had come and gone. She'd only glimpsed Ethan and his *daed* before the three-hour church service commenced. There was no chance to exchange words afterward.

Ready to start her week, she stepped outside and locked

the door. The day promised to be clear and warm, with the slightest hint of a breeze. Barely ten after seven, several hours had yet to pass before her shop was due to open. The time would give her a chance to run a few errands. Basket lodged in the crook of one arm, she set off at a brisk pace. Despite the early hour, the Main Street merchants were already hard at work.

Greeting several and exchanging pleasantries, Amity crossed the street. Turning a corner, she continued to her destination. Part of the original settlement, the sturdy little building housing the post office had originally been a general store. Meticulously maintained for nearly a century, it was a popular stop for tourists.

Her box was crammed full. A sigh winnowed past her lips as she sorted through the tangle of junk mail and flyers. She'd rented the box to keep her private correspondence just that. Private.

A single envelope was lying at the bottom of the pile.

Heart beating double time, she blinked. It was a real letter, addressed in the familiar block lettering most Amish learned in school. The style often carried over into adulthood. To preserve her anonymity, she'd used her middle name, Beth, and her *mamm's* maiden name when she'd placed the ad. The letter was, indeed, addressed to *Miss Beth Spangler*.

"Oh, my."

Her first impulse was to tear it open. Forcing herself to calm down, she decided not to. No reason to be too anxious or eager.

She tucked the envelope in her basket and walked back to her business. The *kaffeeshop* brimmed with customers. Tables were packed with folks working on their laptops or browsing their cell phones.

Amity glanced around with satisfaction. The free internet

was a hit. The idea to extend seating into the shared foyer was her idea. She'd set up the extra tables to entice folks into taking notice of her shop. It worked. People often popped in out of curiosity. Discovering a trove of handmade Amish crafts and other delicacies, browsers turned into buyers. Orders were also coming in via the website.

Vindicated, she slid into an empty seat. Sophie and Emily wouldn't arrive until nine. Bursting with curiosity, she finally opened her letter. She unfolded two sheets of plain paper and read...

My dear Miss Spangler,
Greetings from a faithful reader of our local paper. In perusing the personals, I saw your ad and found it intriguing enough to venture a reply...

The note went on in a most complimentary manner. Hands shaking more than a little, Amity read the note from beginning to end twice more. Though the writer didn't share any personal details right away, he did express hope she'd reply. To close his missive, he'd signed himself Lew C.

Do I know him?

Racking her brain, she tried to think who the writer might be. The name seemed oddly familiar. Was it Lewellyn Christopher? A blacksmith by trade, he often came to the ranch to re-shoe the horses. Nearing forty, he dressed in overalls and wore his blond hair in a short bowl-style cut. His eyes and nose were narrow, and his chin jutted. He was by no means a handsome man. But he was a kind one, who greeted everyone as a friend and smiled often.

Not exactly her type. But then again, perhaps it wasn't Lewellyn who'd written. Could it be Lewis Coblentz? There were at least three other fellows she knew who had those initials. Could one of the men be her mystery correspondent?

She examined the envelope. The return address was also a post office box. Just ten steps away from hers. It was possible she'd even crossed paths with the author of the letter.

Torn in half by her jumbling thoughts, she gazed at the page. A conundrum presented itself. What to do? Answer the letter? Or not?

"Guten morgen," a familiar voice greeted in *Deitsch.*

Amity tilted her head back, stopping when her gaze connected with Ethan Zehr's smiling face. Sturdy as an oak, he towered over her. Hair pushed back from his strong brow, a shopkeeper's apron covered his white shirt and black trousers. "It's nice to see you today."

Amity's insides did a slow backflip. Ethan's steely gaze perfectly complemented his rough-hewn features. He'd trimmed his beard, too, smoothing the scraggly length. The neater, shorter style suited his strong jawline.

She drew a breath to calm her fluttering pulse. "It's *gut* to see you, too."

"Am I disturbing you?" His gaze traveled to the pages in her hand. "If you'd rather not be bothered—"

"It's nothing. An exchange of pleasantries with a *gentleman-freund.*"

A brief shadow flitted across his face. "Oh? You have an admirer?"

For some odd reason, she felt as if he'd caught her redhanded. "An acquaintance," she explained. "We're getting to know each other."

"Not much of a way to get to know someone."

Caught short, she bristled. "I don't recall asking for your opinion."

"What I meant to say is, back in my day if a fella wanted

to get to know a *fraulein*, he'd get out the courting buggy and ask her to take a ride."

"Ah. I see." Plucking out the verbal thorn he'd thrust at her, she pushed it back. "Well, you are quite old. I hate to break it to you, but times have changed. Progressive young folks do things differently nowadays. We can communicate without needing a horse as a chaperone." Shaking her head, she returned the pages to the envelope. "There's a lot to be said for exchanging letters. Writing is the mark of a literate, intelligent mind. You get to know a person. What they like, how they think."

"I can write," he mumbled, wagging a finger toward the letter. "I just don't like to."

"I couldn't care less." She returned a narrow smile. "If you don't mind, I'll see after my concerns, thank you very much." She tucked the precious envelope back into her basket. If she'd needed an incentive to answer her mystery correspondent, he'd given her one.

As for Ethan, every time she thought she liked the man, he did something that put her off.

The goodwill she felt toward him evaporated. Silence hung between them. They were back to square one. He needed to stay on his side of the building. And she would stay on hers.

Don't give him the satisfaction of knowing he'd put a burr under your saddle. Stand up and walk away.

Pushing her chair back, she reached for her basket. Keeping a distance from each other was probably the only way they'd ever get along.

Ethan gave himself a mental thump. What was the matter with him?

He glanced around, relieved their conversation hadn't attracted unwanted attention from customers. He'd intended to have a friendly conversation with Amity Schroder. Instead, he'd stuck his foot straight into his mouth. He hadn't meant to offend. Not at all.

Eager to make amends, he laid a hand on her arm. "Please, don't walk off angry. I didn't mean my words to come out the way they did."

Amity shook off his touch but didn't walk away. Crossing her arms protectively, she regarded him from head to toe and back again. "That's not the way it sounded to me." Pulling her trim little figure stiff and straight, she tipped up her chin. Defiance flared in the depths of her expressive eyes. "Every time I talk to you, I get the feeling you're judging me for not being Amish enough. Well, I can't help how I am or how our church does things in Burr Oak."

He winced. Ouch. The verbal lashing she'd returned was pointed and direct.

"Hey, get this," a voice said from behind. "An Amish smackdown."

Heads turned. People pointed. By now, customers were taking notice of their spat. A few aimed smartphones to record the incident.

Oh, great. What a great way to represent the Plain community. He might have accepted the internet and its intrusions, but that didn't mean he had to like it. He didn't understand why people had to record and upload everything. Some things were personal and best left unrecorded.

Stepping in, he leaned closer. People might watch, but at least they wouldn't hear every word. "I wanted to tell you we're going to be moving."

Amity's expression shifted. Surprise replaced anger. "You are?"

"*Ja.* To the Klatch farm."

"You bought it?"

"*Nein.* Not me. My money is tied up in the *kaffeeshop.*"

"Then who?"

"*Daed.* After visiting with Giles and looking around, he said the farm was exactly where he wanted to be."

Her stern expression melted. "I'm happy he liked it."

"*Ja.* He did. I'm grateful we got it," he said. "*Daed* was born and raised in the country. So was I. And so were my *youngies.* Town living—" he fisted his hands to express his frustration "—hasn't been *gut* for any of us."

"I know being here hasn't been easy. I prayed *Gott* would lead you to a path that would bring healing to your *familie.*"

"I believe it. I wanted you to hear the *gute nachrichten* first. In a roundabout way, you were the one who made it all happen."

"I did nothing. It was all the Lord's work."

Ethan gazed into her face. Once again, she'd proven her beauty went far beyond physical appearance.

"Anyway, it'll take about a month to finalize the paperwork. Since Giles and Jenna will need the time to get packed and moved, it's not a problem."

"I'm glad it worked out."

"*Gott* willing, we will find our way. It'll be better for Liam, I know. Living and working out of town will keep him away from those hooligans who've been leading him wrong. He'll start working at the ranch after we move."

Amity nibbled her bottom lip. "If you're looking for a reliable worker, you could talk to Netha Oberholtzer's *sohn,* Ollie. He has an electric scooter. He's seventeen and on his *rumspringa,* so he is allowed to have it." Giving a cautious smile, she added, "Baptized youths may use them, too. I hope that doesn't upset you too much."

"All I care about is knowing he can do the job. I'll take the recommendation and get in touch with Netha."

"She works at Klein's Market part-time," she added helpfully. "You can reach her there."

"I'll make the call," he promised. "I'll also be hiring another set of hands when Charity goes back to school. If you know anyone…"

He didn't get a chance to finish. Movement inside Amity's shop caught his eye through the wide picture window. Entering through the rear door, her staff began to filter in for the day's work. Lights came on. One of the clerks turned the sign sitting in the window from *Closed* to *Open*. Catching sight of her employer, she raised a hand in greeting.

"Guten morgen," Sophie mouthed through the glass, tossing out a smile.

Amity waved back. "The time's gotten away from me."

Ethan glanced through the shared foyer. The morning rush was over. Customers began to abandon the tables, leaving behind trash that needed to be cleared. Inside his own shop, *Daed* supervised while Charity wiped down the counter. Liam had conveniently made himself scarce.

He checked his pocket watch. Ten after nine. "You're right."

"I have to go." Amity repositioned her basket on her arm, preparing to walk away. "Please congratulate Wayne on his purchase. I hope you are all happy in your new home." Offering a polite nod, she walked away.

Ethan stared in her wake. Consternation knitted his brow. Having spent pleasant time in her company, he'd planned to ask her on a walkabout. Finding out she had a correspondent of the male persuasion had thrown him off his game. While she hadn't said as much, the way she'd tucked the letter between the pages of her Bible indicated she considered it important. For sure and for certain, the fellow had her attention.

Was it serious? Were they courting? She'd given no clues. Should he step up? Or back off?

Nothing ventured. Nothing gained.

Ethan hurried after her, passing beneath the threshold to enter her shop.

Both clerks frowned. The computer tech scowled. He'd walked into their territory, and they didn't like it. Not one bit.

Amity's eyebrows rose into a question. "Did you need something?"

Ethan nervously scrubbed a hand through his hair. It wasn't in his nature to admit he was wrong. But *Daed* had recently broached the subject of expanding the business to sell his *kaffe* blends online. He didn't have the knowledge to make a sound decision one way or another. But he knew who would.

"I didn't get the chance to ask about it, but I'd hoped you have a moment to answer some questions about the internet."

Her guarded expression lightened.

"You can certainly ask," Amity said. "I'll do my best to answer, though Noah would probably be the one you would want to speak to about the technical side."

Noah snorted. "More complaints, I'll bet." He shot Ethan an irritated look.

Amity hushed her employee. "Noah, please."

Ethan offered a feeble smile. No doubt his constant complaints had gotten on the tech's nerves. But like any reasonable man, he was willing to change his mind. To make compromises. Giving customers what they wanted made sense. *Daed* wanted to take things a step further, branching out into online sales. It wouldn't hurt to make a few inquiries, get some facts and figures. Anything he decided on wouldn't happen overnight, but it would give him a cornerstone to build on.

"*Nein.* I'm not here to make a fuss." Hoping he didn't sound like a fool, he laid out what *Daed* had in mind.

Listening intently, the tech nodded. "If you have the time and money to invest, I'd say it's all doable."

"Why don't you take a look at what Noah has set up for us?" Amity invited.

"I'd like that."

"Come, I'll show you a few things." Making a motion with his hand, Noah indicated the back office.

Amity came, too.

The arrangement was simple. A desk, counter space and materials for packing and shipping merchandise were arranged in an efficient layout. The computer, phone and other electronics all had their place.

Noah sat down at the desk, then tapped out some letters on a keyboard. "Here's the website I set up," he explained as images populated the large screen. "It tells who we are, what we sell, and allows customers to place orders."

Ethan bent close. The website had been designed to reflect the decor of the store itself. Simple, old-fashioned and very Amish. "That's impressive."

Noah beamed. "Given what you've told me, it wouldn't be hard to set up something similar for the *kaffeeshop*. You could start small, offering your blends for sale in-store and online. I'd say start with a limited edition, so you'll have a chance to play around with a brand name—a logo and packaging without making a large commitment in volume right away."

"That makes sense."

"It will also give you a chance to gauge sales and adjust accordingly based on demand," Noah suggested, sketching out rough figures and numbers as he spoke. The young man's knowledge was impressive. And persuasive.

"You can manage all this?"

Noah grinned. "*Ja*. Easily."

"Noah has a sharp mind," Amity said. "Coming from Amish, he understands our needs."

"Amity was one of the first to hire me," the tech confirmed. "The majority of Plain folks aren't ready for the digital world. But when they are, I'll be there to help them."

Ethan nodded. Noah had explained things in a way that clicked. A year ago, he wouldn't have considered needing anything like the internet or a computer.

A yelp from the front of the store interrupted. "Noah, help me with the credit card machine!"

Amity waved a hand. "Go help her."

"Ja." Abandoning his desk, Noah hurried out of the office.

"Sorry—Emily always has trouble getting it to connect," Amity said, explaining the issue.

"I still get fuzzled with ours," Ethan admitted. "But I'm trying to learn." A little uncertain, he added, "That's *gut*, right?"

"It's a start."

"I'm not sure I could explain it all to *Daed*. If you wouldn't mind, maybe you could come over tonight and—" His words evaporated, halted by the humorous smile tickling her lips.

Amity set her hands on her hips. "Why, Ethan Zehr," she declared, and her bright gaze snapped with mischief. "Are you asking me out?"

Chapter Seven

"It's not a date. Amity's just coming over to talk about what it'll take to put the *kaffeeshop* online. That's what you wanted. To expand the business."

"Then why are you putting on a fuss about cleaning up?" Eyes twinkling, *Daed* closed his Bible. "And cooking a meal?"

Setting aside the broom and dustpan, Ethan rolled the living room rug back into place. "Wanting the house to be decent and having a home-cooked meal has nothing to do with Amity."

"Is that so?"

"Aye. No sense in living like pigs in a sty. And we have to eat. I don't know about you, but I've had enough cold cuts to last a lifetime."

Daed tipped back his head, sniffing the air. "You're sure Charity can handle the cooking?"

Ethan glanced toward the attached kitchenette. "I'm sure she can handle a pot of spaghetti," he said. "All she has to do is fry the meat, boil the pasta and pour the sauce on it. And it's not hard to spread some garlic butter on bread and toast it."

"If you say so," *Daed* mumbled under his breath.

Ethan shot a frown. Like most Amish girls, Charity had been put to work in the kitchen at a young age. However, his *tochter's* skills at the stove weren't the best. He often forced himself to eat what she served to avoid hurting her feelings.

"Maybe you should do the cooking if you think you can do better."

Daed visibly blanched. "*Ach*, no. The kitchen belongs to women, as it should." Not fond of his *enkelin's* cooking, the old man often ambled down to the senior center to join the old folks for a meal and a game of checkers. The *Englisch* ladies there served a nice spread, and he usually came home with leftovers.

"Don't be hard on her. She's trying her best." True, he'd lost a pound or two and his pants were loose. But so far, everyone had survived.

Shamed by his remark, *Daed* stroked his long beard. "Suppose you're right. The Lord tells us not to be quarrelsome and to be kind to everyone." Nevertheless, he grimaced. "If only the girl would learn to make a decent biscuit."

Ethan silently shook his head. Charity's attempts at sourdough hadn't always been a success. The starter had gone moldy more than once.

"Dinner will be fine. There's not much to be ruined opening a can of sauce."

"If you say so…" *Daed's* doubtful words trailed into silence. Conversation thankfully fell into a lull.

After fluffing a few throw pillows, Ethan smoothed the wrinkles out of the afghan covering the back of the sofa. His throat tightened as he looked at the blanket. Though worn and a little frayed, he refused to part with it. His young bride had made the knitted throws after they'd married. Bedridden through her difficult pregnancies, Priscilla had kept herself busy. Her skilled fingers had created colorful patterns out of the yarn. Both of their *kinder* had been swaddled in it at one time or another. Holding her little one close, Priscilla would hum a gentle lullaby to put the *boppli* to sleep. Those times, so peaceful and perfect, were ones he'd always cherish.

Satisfied he'd done a decent job, he couldn't say he'd be sorry to leave the apartment behind. Arranged for efficiency and not comfort, the kitchen and living room were barely adequate. Three small bedrooms, a washroom and a walk-in utility closet meant everyone was living elbow-to-elbow. As they were short a bedroom, he made do by sleeping on the sofa. At night, it folded out into a bed. By day, the bedding was tucked away.

He hoped getting back into a *haus*, a real home, would help ease everyone's frayed nerves.

If only Tanner Dekker hadn't sold the other half of the building out from under him, he'd have more space for the *kaffeeshop* and a second unit to rent. As it stood, he'd have to be satisfied with the gains he'd made. Business was steady and his options to grow were viable. The steps were small, but success was like running a marathon. Slow and steady would win the race.

The hard work will pay off, he reminded himself. *Whatever I do, I must do in the name of the Lord Jesus.* The thought gave him comfort and encouragement. Go forward. Go on. Take another step. Tomorrow was full of promise.

Peeking into the kitchen, he checked on Charity. Clad in her usual day clothes, she padded around on bare feet. Wearing no *kapp*, a single long braid of hair hung down her back. She opened a package and dumped the pasta into a large pot of boiling water, then added a pinch of salt and covered it with a lid. A baguette of French bread sat on the counter, waiting to be sliced and buttered for toasting. She'd even grated some cheese to sprinkle on top.

"Everything okay, sweetie? Do you need any help?"

"I've got it." Adding a dash of salt and pepper, she used

a spatula to turn the ground beef and chopped onions sizzling in a cast-iron skillet. Instead of homemade sauce, hers was store-bought.

"Just checking."

"I can handle it." Turning from the stove, Charity ran hot water over the dishes in the sink. She washed them by hand, stacking each neatly in the dish rack.

Ethan smiled with pride. Fine-boned and slender, with thick blond hair and high cheekbones, Charity was the spitting image of her *mamm*. He still hadn't gotten used to seeing her doing a grown woman's chores. On the cusp of thirteen, she'd soon be done with school. Come fifteen, she'd be old enough to walkabout with young men. Soon—too soon—he'd have to let her go.

"It's not fair for you to do everything, I'll send Liam to help. He can dry the dishes and set the table."

"Okay." Returning to the stove, she flipped on the oven to heat. "He can help me with the broiler. I just want to toast the bread."

"I'll get him."

Leaving Charity to her cooking, Ethan walked down the short hall. A sliver of light showed beneath the door to Liam's bedroom.

Pausing, he cocked his head. Inside, he heard voices. Surprising, because he expected his *sohn* to be alone. *What's he gotten into now?*

After turning the knob, he poked his head inside. Liam sat on his bed. A small object was cradled in his hands.

Ethan stepped inside. "What have you got?"

Caught in the act, Liam tried to hide the contraband by shoving it under his pillow.

"It's nothing."

"I know what I saw." Ethan extended a hand, palm up. "Let me have it."

Swallowing hard, Liam retrieved the object. Rising, he gave up a smartphone.

"Where did you get this?" Suspicion flooded from all sides. Liam's pending criminal charge weighed heavily on his mind. Given that it was a first offense, Sheriff Miller reckoned Liam would get off with a fine and a warning... if he stayed out of trouble. "How long have you had it? Did you steal it?"

"I didn't steal it. I bought it a few weeks ago. With my own money." Pausing, he added in a rush, "Lots of kids have them. Even Amish ones."

"I heard voices. Who were you talking to?"

"I wasn't talking to anyone. I was looking at videos."

Ethan eyed the offensive device. "Such as?" Back in Augsberger, Bishop Swarey often preached about the dangers of electronics in the hands of the community's youths. He didn't want to imagine what Liam might be searching out online.

"Seth was telling me about the rodeo and some of the events he competes in. I wanted to see what they were, so I looked on the internet." Giving a nervous look, Liam's hand scraped his face. The barest traces of stubble were beginning to shadow his upper lip and sideburns. "I'm a *gut* rider. I think it's something I'd like to do."

Surprise lifted Ethan's eyebrows. The county fair and rodeo were popular summer events in Oklahoma. The Amish often attended both. Women enjoyed entering their needlework and cooking in the contests. Men showed their woodworking crafts or livestock. Liam often raised goats and lambs to sell at the junior livestock auctions. But Priscilla had put her foot down and said no when Liam showed an interest in arena sports.

"You think you're *gut* enough?"

Liam shrugged weakly. "*Nee*, not yet." A slew of emotions crossed his face even as ambition flared in his eyes. "But I could be. Seth said he'd teach me everything he knows. He does barrel racing and calf roping. And Levi and that older *Englisch* man—I think his name's Ezra—they've trained a lot of fellows to compete."

Nodding, Ethan gave his *sohn* a long look. "I think you should."

Liam released a soft breath of relief. "I can do it. You wait and see."

The tension between them eased.

As for the smartphone…

Before they'd moved to Burr Oak, Ethan never would have considered letting either of his *youngies* own one. But the Texas Amish were different. He'd seen more than one Amish kid with the devices, and no one seemed to think anything about it. Given that he was about to dip a toe into technology himself, did he have the right to restrict Liam from owning a phone? As Amish *kinder* were not under the authority of the church, they were given certain allowances during *rumspringa*. Maybe there was a use for the thing after all. But Liam would have to prove he was responsible enough to have it.

"Because you were not honest with me, you may not have the phone."

"But, *Datt*!"

Ethan raised his hand. "Let me finish. Privileges aren't given. They're earned. If you want the phone, you are going to have to show me you're mature enough to have it. That means doing your job and staying out of trouble with the law. Show me you can do that, and I will reconsider letting you have it."

Liam nodded. "That's fair." He thought for a moment. "How long?"

"Six months."

"Promise?"

"I'm a man of my word. Now, show me you're a man of yours."

Liam grinned and drew back his shoulders, sitting straighter. "Deal!"

"I'll hang on to this." Ethan tucked the cell into his back pocket. "I hope you saved a little of your money. You'll still be paying to fix your bicycle."

"I have enough to pay for repairs. I know Charity's been wanting it, so I'm giving it to her." Puffing up a little, he added, "I won't need it since I'll be working at the ranch. Riding horses and stuff."

Guilt prodded Ethan hard. Focused on the problems with Liam, he'd practically ignored Charity. She'd gotten nothing to enjoy. He'd even said no to the kitten she'd begged to keep, saying she was too busy to care for the animal.

"Sounds like a fine idea. I know Charity would like to have the bike." Once they got settled in their new place, he'd allow her to have a cat. The felines living in the Klatches' barn probably had several litters a year. It wouldn't be hard to catch and tame a few for indoor living.

"It'll be good as new. I promise."

Thankful the matter was settled, Ethan put his hand on his *sohn's* shoulder. "You've made mistakes, but I'm proud you want to do better."

Liam offered an unexpected hug. "I didn't mean to be bad." Choking back a sob, he sniffled. "I—I miss *Mamm* so much."

Ethan's throat tightened as he returned the embrace. "I miss her, too," he returned quietly.

"I'll do better, I promise. I'll make you proud. Just wait and see."

"I believe you." Stepping back, Ethan awkwardly cleared his throat. "I almost forgot—Charity needs your help in the kitchen. She wants to toast some bread in the broiler."

"She always turns it too high." Exiting his room, Liam disappeared down the hall.

Ethan watched him go. As he did, it dawned on him the Lord had answered his prayer. The dark clouds of rebellion hanging over the moody teen were thinning. The work and focus it took to learn new skills was exactly what Liam needed.

Relief bubbled up. After a rocky patch, it looked like things were beginning to settle down and go right in their lives. He sent up a quick prayer, grateful that *Gott* was steering his *familie* in the right direction.

A buzz at the door reminded him company was expected. He'd invited Amity to supper. Now, she was here. And he wasn't ready.

Amity held back her gasp. When the door opened, she hadn't expected to see a disheveled man standing behind it. Dark curls askew on his head, a few pieces of lint clinging to his thick beard. Sleeves rolled to his elbows, damp stains splotching his shirt. The knees of his trousers were dusty.

"I was to come tonight?" she asked, looking him up and down. "Or am I mistaken?"

Embarrassment reddened Ethan's cheeks. "Aye, you're right on time." He combed his fingers through his hair, attempting to smooth the wild tangle. "I'm the one running late."

"I can come back some other time."

"Not at all. *Daed's* been wanting to talk to you." Stepping back, he opened the door wide.

After passing through a short entryway, Amity stepped into the living room. Arranged comfortably, none of the furniture or other belongings were new. But everything was well kept. Rugs shook out, the floor was spotless. Nary a speck of dust lingered. The cloying scent of onions and garlic mingling with some sort of beef filled the air, reminding her that she hadn't eaten a bite since noon.

"Charity's making supper. I hope you'll stay."

Amity inwardly grumbled. She'd blocked out thirty minutes to visit. No more than that. Puzzling over her mystery correspondent, she was curious to know more. She'd already made up her mind to answer. Her fingers itched to take pen in hand and dash off a reply.

She forced a smile. "I'm looking forward to it." It would be rude to say no. Nor did she want to hurt Charity's feelings.

Laying aside his paper, Wayne Zehr made a move to rise. "*Ach*, you've come."

Amity waved him down. "No need to get up."

"*Daed* has some questions about the café going online." Hovering, Ethan couldn't seem to decide what to do with his hands. He appeared nervous and out of sorts.

Realization pinged her. Ethan was a widower. He'd probably never entertained a single woman in his home without his *ehefrau* present. But they weren't courting and didn't need a chaperone. Did they?

"I'm happy to," she said, slipping off her shawl. As it wasn't a social occasion, she hadn't changed out of her work clothes. Neutral in color, her simple dress had a high neckline and long sleeves. Her apron was cinched around her waist. Were she at home she would have removed it, and her prayer *kapp.* She also would have kicked off her boots, relishing the chance to relax in bare feet.

Ethan awkwardly claimed her shawl. He hung it on a peg near the door. "*Ja.* That sounds *gut.*" Aware he wasn't decent, he brushed a hand down the front of his shirt. "If you don't mind, I'd like to wash up before we eat."

She gave a kind smile. "Of course." Amish men weren't known to bend an elbow when it came to women's chores. He'd worked diligently to present a decent home. It showed he cared about how he kept his *familie.*

"I'll only be a few minutes." Nodding, he disappeared down the hall. The bathroom door shut behind him with a firm click.

Left standing, Amity glanced around. *You don't have to stay more than an hour. Chat a bit, take a quick bite and go.*

"Have a seat, if you like," Wayne Zehr said.

"Danke." Sitting down at the end of the sofa, she folded her hands in her lap.

"Cup of *kaffee*?" the old man asked. "Or tea?"

"Tea would be nice." She didn't want either. She just wanted to go home. Knowing they'd be moving soon was a relief. Now that they'd called a truce, she considered the Zehr *familie* to be pleasant acquaintances. Fine if they spent a little time visiting. But they weren't friends. Nor did she feel inclined to take it any further. Ethan Zehr might be eligible, but he wasn't her type.

"Charity!" Wayne bellowed. "Miss Amity's here. Make some tea."

Charity popped out of the kitchen. "You don't have to yell, *Poppi.*" Tossing an apologetic smile, she scurried away. A minute later she appeared carrying a tray. A cup and saucer sat in the middle. Careful not to spill a drop, she delivered the steeping tea. A bowl of sugar and a small pitcher of cream accompanied a spoon and folded linen napkin.

Amity accepted the cup. A pattern of roses and leaves decorated the fragile porcelain. An antique, it had most likely passed through several generations of Amish women.

"How kind. *Danke.*"

"I remembered you like cream in your tea," Charity said, offering to pour a dollop. "And sugar, too."

"I do," Amity said, stirring in the extras.

"I hope you like spaghetti. The noodles kind of grew and there's a lot." Leaving the tray, Charity returned to her cooking.

Flipping open a notebook, Wayne leaned forward. "Now that you're settled, I wanted to ask about packaging my *kaffee* to sell online. Ethan says the fella you hired might be willing to help us out."

"Noah would be the one to talk to if you are going to sell online. He can set up all you'd need and help manage it, too. His price is reasonable, too."

"I'm glad to hear it, I've been thinking we should expand, but Ethan was always against the notion. And Bishop Swarey always forbid it."

Her eyebrows rose. "Even for business purposes?"

"He doesn't like the idea of bringing in outsiders to do the work. His point of view is that once we started bringing them in, they'd push out our ways to put in their own."

"I take it he doesn't like *Englisch*?"

"*Nein.* He says their ways are no *gut* for Plain folks."

Amity quietly sipped her tea. She couldn't imagine living under such a strict *Ordnung.* But she knew they existed. Some were so old-fashioned and strait-laced that they didn't even allow singing in church. She couldn't imagine sitting like a stone in the pews. On Sundays the Burr Oak congregation sang without restraint, lifting their voices to heaven.

"I'm relieved Bishop Harrison and our *Leit* take an opposing view. The *Englisch* are our brothers and sisters in Christ. The bishop believes we can adapt and use their tools while still maintaining autonomy over our thoughts and actions. If we stay strong in our faith, I believe we will do fine."

"All I can say is Bishop Swarey is old and set in his ways. Some folks feel they're being left behind by not changing with the times."

Amity nodded. "We must be a part of it whether we like it or not."

"Aye. I agree. And Ethan's starting to come around to that way of thinking. It's been a battle, but he's easing up."

Amity chuckled. She liked the way Wayne spoke. Frank and honest, he held nothing back. "Has he always been so tightly wound?"

"*Ja.* He takes after his *mamm*, a hundred percent. I come from New Order myself. Born and raised in Choteau, Oklahoma. But Letha wouldn't marry me unless I resettled in Augsberger, with her side." Sighing heavily, his gaze grew distant with memory. "I was young, and she made my heart happy. Prettiest girl I ever saw."

"It sounds like you found a way to overcome your differences."

The old man snapped back to the present. "Aye. Letha would complain—" he tugged the droopy lobe of one ear "—and I'd pretend I didn't hear. Kept us together 'til the day she left this earth, *Gott* rest her soul."

Ethan strolled into the living room. Dressed in a fresh shirt, suspenders in place, he'd tried to tame his unruly curls. They remained as stubborn as ever, falling every which way.

"What's that about *Mamm*?"

Caught gossiping, the old man's face reddened. "Oh, I was just reminiscing about the old days."

Ethan's lips twitched. "I know exactly what you were saying. *Mamm* was a stick-in-the-mud. And she raised two little sticks just like her."

"Letha was tightly wound," Wayne conceded, folding his arms across his chest. "She never saw the bright side of life. It was always clouds and gloom."

"And she always thought you didn't take things seriously enough," Ethan countered.

"I just followed the Lord's word and cast away my worries." The old man rubbed his hand along his jaw before smoothing his shaggy beard. "Letha always fretted. Not because there were any problems, but because it gave her something to wring her hands over."

A disturbance from the kitchen interrupted. A great clatter was followed by a cry of anguish. "*Ach*, Liam! Look what you made me do!"

Amity jumped to her feet, nearly stepping on Ethan's heel as they both rushed to the kitchen. Charity stood in the center of a mess. A pot was lying at her feet, spilling out pasta and meat sauce. Liam crouched on his knees in front of the oven.

Ethan surveyed the disaster. "What happened?"

Charity burst into tears. "I was just moving the spaghetti off the stove—" overcome with emotion, she began to blubber "—and I slipped."

Liam climbed to his feet. "It's my fault. I was trying to get the broiler lit and she tripped over me."

"I'm sorry." Breath hitching into hiccups, Charity bawled harder. "I didn't mean to."

Gaze shifting over the mess, Ethan put a steadying hand on her shoulder. "It's all right. Accidents happen." He kneeled, setting the pot upright before scooping up the mess.

Charity sniffled. "I wanted to make a nice supper."

"Guess we won't have it tonight," Liam said, snarfing a laugh.

Ethan shot a frown. "Don't."

Liam sobered. "Sorry."

Stepping into the kitchen, Amity snagged a dishcloth to help clean up the sauce. "We've all done it at one time or another. I'm sure it would have been delicious."

Charity sighed, cupping her face in her hands. "I'm so clumsy. I should have known better than to try and step around Liam."

Amity sopped up the red goop. Returning to the sink, she turned on the tap and wrung out the rag. "I can't tell you how many times Gail's burned something on that old stove of hers. And me...why I can't even boil water without ruining it."

"Really?"

"Cooking is a hard job. Sometimes we women just don't get it right."

"Your *mamm* did it, too," Ethan said, dumping the ruined meal into a garbage pail. "I remember when she used salt instead of sugar in her pumpkin pie."

Charity suddenly perked up. "*Ach*, that must have been awful."

"It was." A grimace puckered his mouth. "I didn't want to hurt her feelings, so I ate every bite."

Charity walked to the counter where the rest of the meal waited. "I don't have anything left but the garlic bread."

"Wrap it up for another time. How about we get a pizza?"

A grin wreathed Liam's face. "I could go for that."

"You don't mind, *Datt*?"

A smile found its way into Ethan's eyes. "It won't hurt us to eat out one time."

Amity looked between father and daughter. His patience

and gentleness impressed her. *There's more to him than meets the eye.*

Beneath his stern exterior beat the heart of a man who cared deeply about his *youngies*. That much was clear. Ethan hadn't grumbled once about the mess or wasting food. He'd set to cleaning up without batting an eye. Drama put to rest, the kitchen returned to order.

Knowing the challenges he faced made it easier to forgive the Sturm und Drang over the internet. It also made her that much more open to putting aside their differences. Perhaps someday they could truly be friends.

"Tomatino's Pizza is the best in town," she suggested. "And they deliver."

Chapter Eight

Everyone agreed pizza would be fine for supper. Ordered and devoured, the meal was deemed to be delicious. The evening was enjoyable and included a brief Bible study before settling in for a fun hour of Scrabble. Much to everyone's surprise, Liam was the most engaged. Excited about his new job, he spoke about his intention to start training for the rodeo events he hoped to compete in. The teen wasn't deterred when Ethan cautioned it would take time and practice to qualify. Liam was determined and looked forward to the challenging activity.

At nine o'clock, the gathering wound down. Eyes drooping, the *youngies* yawned. Game over, both shuffled off to brush their teeth and change into nightclothes. There was a brief squabble over who would go first. Charity won because "beauties before beasts." Sticking out her tongue, she shut the door in Liam's face.

"Guess I'll wait." Shrugging, Liam disappeared into his bedroom.

Amity chuckled over their antics. Growing up, she'd shared a washroom with her *schwesters*. Competition to get in first was fierce. As the *kind* stuck not quite in the middle, she'd had to learn to elbow the older girls aside to get a moment alone.

"I can't believe the change in Liam," Ethan said as he

put away the game. "He hasn't smiled once since his *mamm* passed. Now, he's grinning ear to ear."

Reaching for his coffee, Wayne pushed away from the table. "Being back on a horse will do him *gut*. I knew from the beginning living in town wasn't where we belonged."

Ethan sighed. "I know. But it was the best deal I could find at the time. The location worked and the price fit my budget." After putting the lid back on the game, he tucked it in a nearby cabinet. "Now I just need to find more engagement for Charity. I'm worried she's getting left out."

"She's got a quick mind," Amity said. The shy little mouse had the heart of a tiger when challenged. Dictionary in hand, Charity created the most unusual words from her selection of letters.

Pride washed through Ethan's expression. "Charity's always been bright when it comes to learning. She loves to read, and she's smart with words. She wants to publish stories for *kinder* when she's grown."

"I've no doubt she will be a fine writer."

"She's worn two ribbons out on my old Royal typewriter," Wayne said, chuckling.

"She's saving her allowance for one of her own." Ethan exaggerated a grimace. "Guess I'll have to let her have it since Liam has a cell phone."

Surprise creased *Daed's* face. "You found it, did you?"

"You knew he had it? And you didn't say anything?"

"*Ja.* I knew. I might be old, but I was a *youngie* once. I'm fully aware of what *kinder* try to hide from their elders."

"And you know *Mamm* caught us. Every time. I still remember sitting in the corner, reading Psalm 119. We couldn't move until we'd read every verse. Ten times."

"Letha did believe *Gottesschwert* should be memorized

through regular reading if was going to make an impact on your character."

"That. And the fact she backed it up with a fierce look."

"Letha could give a scowl that would freeze water. Can't say I didn't get a few myself."

Amity laughed. "All *mamms* can do that. I know mine could."

Ethan arched an eyebrow. "She would have scowled for sure, knowing you're keeping secrets. If I'd have known—"

The old man returned a disgruntled huff. "You wouldn't have let him have it and there would have been another argument."

"Not necessarily. But I do think Liam should have asked permission first. Then, we would have sat down and discussed it."

"I suppose you're right," *Daed* conceded. "*Gott* says he who makes his ways crooked will be found out."

"Exactly. And we do live by the Lord's word, as best we can." Ethan pulled the cell out of his back pocket. "I took the phone."

The old man's eyes widened. "And he didn't throw a hissy?"

"*Nein.* I told him if he wanted it, he'd have to earn the privilege. He has six months to prove he can stay out of trouble."

Daed visibly relaxed. "That sounds fair."

Ethan tucked the phone in a nearby drawer. "I believe going to work at the ranch will be the best thing for him."

"Another thing you can thank Amity for," *Daed* said.

"Finding a place Liam wants to work is a blessing." Glancing her way, a smile curved Ethan's lips. "I'm thankful every day for your help." Admiration glimmered in his eyes. His compliment was genuine, spoken with sincerity.

Amity's cheeks heated. "I'm happy to know Liam's looking forward to it," she said, reluctant to accept the praise.

Ethan reached for the thermal carafe on the table. "Care for a refill?"

She covered her empty cup with a hand. "If I have another, I'll not get a wink."

"I should probably skip it, too. I'm jittery enough as it is. And five in the morning comes early."

"I have to get up early, too." Preparing to depart, Amity rose. She reached for her shawl, then wound it around her shoulders. "If you don't mind, I'll bid you all *gute nacht*."

Ethan set down the carafe. "I'll see you home."

"*Ach*, not to worry. I think I'm safe walking from your door to mine." She waved a dismissive hand. "It's just a few steps away."

"I'd like a walk. Give me a chance to stretch my legs."

She considered. "I could use the exercise."

"You two go on," *Daed* urged.

Ethan accompanied her to the door. Reaching for his hat, he plunked it on his head and followed her outside. The door shut behind them with a firm click.

Stepping to the rail, she drew in a breath. The crisp night air was refreshing. The view from the balcony placed them directly under the clear night sky. Stars twinkled like diamonds spread across black velvet.

Ethan paid it no mind. Descending into silence, his mind seemed to wander elsewhere.

"Is something wrong?"

He thought a moment before answering. "I'm still bothered *Daed* didn't tell me about Liam's phone. I should know what's happening under my roof. Liam should have been honest and asked permission to have it."

"Would you let him keep it?"

"I'd have said *nein*."

"If he were younger, I'd agree with you."

"But?"

"He's nearing *rumspringa* and it's natural for him to want what the others his age have."

"I guess it's pointless trying to keep those gadgets away from our *kinder*." Frustration chuffed past his lips. "Might as well just hand all the *youngies* what they want and turn them loose."

Amity couldn't help chuckling. "There's another solution."

Ethan returned a doubtful look. "And that is?"

"Teach them to use them wisely. In an emergency, a phone can be a lifesaver. Working at the ranch, Liam will need to be able to communicate with the other hands. Used that way, it's a tool. He doesn't have to be glued to it like other kids are."

"I suppose that makes sense." Shoving his hands in his pockets, Ethan scraped his boot against the iron railing. "I know Liam wanted to fit in. He's never been around *Englisch* kids before. He wants what they have. And I've heard how people talk when they think we're not listening."

"We all hear the same thing," she said. "They call us backward. Out of step. Ignorant. Hard for an Amish kid to ignore, wouldn't you say?"

"Ja."

"We both know it's hard to be Plain. And the *Englisch* keep moving in. It's why Bishop Harrison keeps a close eye on what technology we use and how we use it. He knows temptation is there. It's why he had the community center added to the church."

Ethan leaned forward, propping his elbows on the railing. "When I first moved here, I didn't understand the need for such a large building." His brow furrowed. "It seemed like the bishop was a bit of a braggart about the size of his flock."

"Oh, not at all! There were indeed naysayers who said Clark Harrison was spending too much money when he proposed adding a youth and community center. But once people saw how beneficial it was, tongues stopped wagging. Now, the *Leit* hosts most everything there, including bake sales and auctions. And the offices are a base for charity projects. Oh, and there are work frolics and game nights, too."

"You've convinced me. I didn't realize how useful a place like that would be."

"I know you haven't lived in Burr Oak long. To an outsider, it might seem we're more permissive, but we're not. Ours is a close-knit community. We care about each other and keep an eye on neighbors."

His tense manner eased. "I know that to be true. You lent a hand when you didn't have to. You could have turned a blind eye to Liam's troubles after the flack I gave you."

"When I looked at him, I saw Levi. He was struggling, too, when he came to the ranch. His whole *familie* was gone in an accident and he had no one. He even tried to run away a time or two." She chuckled. "But my *daadi* kept going and getting him. He knew a young man needed the focus of hard work and responsibility, so he put Levi to work with the cattle. And even though he left the community, Levi did come back. Now, he's raising his *kinder* in the faith with the same values. I've no doubt they won't grow into fine young people. Given a chance, I believe Liam will, too."

"I'm relieved he's getting along with Seth. I didn't mind him having *Englisch freundes*, but the group he hung out with were troublemakers."

"Amish and *Englisch* folks mix well here. For the most part, they respect our ways. And we are open to accepting theirs as long as we can retain our faith and traditions. Still, there are a few bad apples in every barrel."

"True."

"And I agree with Sheriff Miller. Liam needs some distance from temptation. Seth is close to his age, and they share common interests."

"Don't know how I feel about the rodeo business." Doubt drew down the corners of Ethan's mouth. "I know they're popular and *youngies* do compete in the sport. But it seems dangerous."

"Aye. It is. But we can't shield our *kind* from danger all their lives. Anything can happen in the blink of an eye. All we can do is pray for protection. *Gott* says He gives his angels charge to guard us as we walk."

"I know the Lord's word." Throat visibly working, Ethan's expression darkened. "I also know that sometimes prayers aren't answered. I'll never understand why we lose people we love before their time. I don't know if I could take it if something happened to Liam or Charity."

Struck by his willingness to speak openly about his private fears, Amity gazed into his haunted eyes. Ethan's loss of his *ehefrau* was still very much on his mind. In public, he wore a stone face. In private, his inner walls came down to reveal a gentle nature and soft heart.

It was only natural he'd be more protective of his *kinder*. She'd never had *youngies* of her own. But she'd been around enough to know how they should be raised. With care and caution, true enough. However, they also needed positive outlets that engaged their energy and interests. Bumps, scrapes and setbacks all came with the territory of growing up.

"If you say no, Liam might be safer. But he'd be like a caged bird. If he can't live, can't stretch his wings, how will he learn to fly?"

How do I let go?
Lips pressed tight, Ethan lowered his head. When he'd moved his *familie* to Burr Oak, he'd known there would be

changes. The location, the church and the community itself were all different. He'd convinced himself he was up to the challenge.

But he wasn't. Not really. Despite leaning on his faith, he felt so alone. Fear, doubt and worry gnawed on his nerves like a hungry animal. More than anything, he missed Priscilla. Her gentle voice and soft hugs never failed to calm his unquiet mind.

He'd accepted that she was gone. That his life would never be the same. But knowing it and understanding it didn't ease the ache. Or the emptiness.

Drawing a breath, he steadied himself against the onslaught of emotions. Loss was like a wound. Keep picking the scab and it would never heal. The bandage he'd put on his heart had to stay in place. Though deeply scarred, he hoped it would someday beat again.

You must go forward, he reminded himself. Yesterday was a memory. Tomorrow was an adventure, yet to be explored.

"You're right," he said, breaking his brief silence. "Life comes with risks. Liam will have to choose his path. And I'll have to pray harder."

"We all make mistakes when we're young. We stumble. We fall. If it makes you feel any better, Levi isn't going to hand Liam a rope and turn him loose. Liam might know how to ride, but training and practice will teach him safety and make him a better horseman."

Assurance soothed his concern. "I'll not stand in Liam's way if it's something he wants to do."

"Gut." Satisfaction widened her grin. "Now that we've settled that, what about Charity? You mentioned you were concerned she was getting left out."

Guilt pinged hard. Even though he didn't intend it, his youngest always got the short end of the stick. Liam was always the squeaky wheel, needing the most attention. Quiet and obedient, Charity's needs usually got brushed aside.

"I am. But I don't know what to do with her. She spends hours at the library. And she's looking forward to going back to school and making new friends. But that's over a month away." He spread his hands. "What else can she do?"

"She can join my sewing circle. And since she likes to read, you could put her in the book club for teen girls. Evie Ledbretch hosts it at the community center. The books are age-appropriate, and the girls often have some lively discussions."

"Sounds like something Charity would enjoy."

"I have something else on my mind, too."

He blinked. "I don't understand." *What else could there be?*

"A man wouldn't. But Charity is twelve. I've heard her talking with Emily and Sophie. I know she has questions, but they aren't sure how to answer her because they're afraid you'd disapprove."

"Answers about what?"

Amity cleared her throat in a meaningful manner. "Girl things."

Heat flamed in Ethan's face. Embarrassed, he dropped his gaze. Um, okay. Game. Set. Match. Amity had claimed the points and victory was hers. Her concern was valid. He wouldn't feel comfortable discussing things like that with his daughter. The groups would offer a safe space for Charity to learn what to expect when it came to a young lady's private concerns.

"Priscilla started to educate her about that," he explained. "But her health wasn't the best. There were days when she couldn't get out of bed because she was so weak." The words left his mouth before he realized he'd said them. Since arriving in Burr Oak, he hadn't talked much about life in Oklahoma. All folks knew was that he'd lost his *ehefrau.* They didn't know how or why, and he'd never been inclined to share any details.

Her stern facade melted. "*Ach*, I understand," she said softly. "My *mamm* was sick before she passed. Had the cancer, she did. I was about Charity's age when she left us."

"I'm sorry to hear that. It must have been hard on your *familie*."

"It was. But I had Gail and Rebecca to teach me. We all had to grow up a little faster." Speaking softly, her gaze grew distant.

"Did you still have your *vater*?" he asked.

"We did." She briefly worried her lower lip before continuing. "And he made sure we all got on with the business of living. But he was never happy. And he never smiled again. He mourned *Mamm* until the day he died."

Ethan knew the feeling. "I don't think the ones we've lost ever leave our minds."

"They don't. I think about *Mamm* and *Daadi* every day. At first, I was sad. For them. And for myself. But I'm not anymore."

"Why is that?"

Amity tipped back her head, searching the sky. "Because I know they are in heaven." Without missing a beat, she switched to *Deitsch*. "*Sie gehörten Gott, und sie sind zu hause.*"

Her simple words were touching. *They belonged to Gott, and they are at home.*

The brief eulogy was perfect. No more words were needed. They stood in silence, reluctant to break the connection of mutual support and understanding. The moment was precious. A gift from one soul reaching out to another.

"I didn't mean to get all sad and moody." She offered a tentative smile. "Still want to go on that walk?"

"*Ja*, I do."

They descended to street level. The narrow alley behind the building crossed into a back lot that served as extra parking space. Past the lot was another street. A crosswalk led to the park. Come sundown, proprietors who lived above their shops would gather to socialize after a long day. Tonight, the entire place was deserted. Not a soul could be seen.

Without voicing a destination, they began to walk. After crossing the street, they strolled down a stone path winding through the grassy knoll. At its end was a rest area populated with swings and monkey bars. Sturdy benches offered a place to sit. Illumination from nearby lampposts chased away the shadows, offering safety and security.

"Shall we sit?" he asked. "Or would it be untoward at this late hour?"

"Oh, I think we're fine." Amity sat, smoothing the folds of her white apron across her lap. "If I worried about what people thought, I'd fret all day."

Ethan took the opposite end of the bench, careful to keep a discrete distance. "I have to admit Bishop Swarey would raise his eyebrows if he saw us sitting alone at night."

"*Gut* thing he's not here," she teased. "He'd be scandalized if he saw you with me."

"I had no idea you were a lady who garnered gossip."

She lifted a hand, ticking off her fingers as she spoke. "Twenty-five. Unwed. Living alone. Those three things right there peg me as a spinster who has no hope of finding an *ehmann*." Grimacing a little, she added, "Also my mouth sometimes gets the better of me. But you know that."

"Aye. You have ragged my ear a time or two."

"I'm determined to get my way. I often do." She pressed out a heavy sigh. "To my detriment."

"I've noticed you don't hold back when you have something to say."

"The bishop has warned me I'm too overbearing. He says no man wants a quarrelsome woman. I guess he's right."

"But you're not inclined to change?"

"Nein. I'm a sow's ear and not a silk purse, but that's the way *Gott* made me. And I know most Amish men want a delicate *mädchen.* One who flutters her lashes and blushes behind her hand." Hands dropping into her lap, her expression grew wistful. "I've never been like that. I never will be." Her smile wavered a little. "It's probably why no one's asked me to marry. I'm too stubborn and independent. I always want to do things for myself." Though she attempted to make light of the matter, there was a hint of longing behind her words.

"That fella you're writing. Is he anyone special?"

She blinked. "I'm surprised you recalled that."

"I pay more attention than you think I do."

She paused a moment before answering. "I've only gotten one letter so far. But it was quite sweet."

Curiosity prodded. "You planning to write back?"

She laughed. *"Ja.* I think I will." Crossing her fingers, she comically bit her lower lip. Her nose scrunched in the cutest way. "Who knows? This might be *the one.*"

As they conversed, Ethan's fingers nervously intertwined with the edge of his suspenders. He tried to suppress the pounding of his heart, but it was futile. The realization dawned on him like the first light of a new day. He was jealous another fellow had caught her interest. The newfound emotion was exhilarating. And terrifying. Her hopes reflected his own yearnings. The ice chilling his emotions had, at long last, begun to thaw.

"Daed thinks I should start courting again."

Her gaiety sobered. "And how do you feel about that?"

"The idea scares me. Priscilla was the only girl I ever dated. Never been with anybody else." As he spoke, Ethan ran a hand down his beard. Aside from recently giving it a trim to tame the scraggly overgrowth, he didn't dare cut it off. He wasn't prepared to take things that far. Not yet. "Anyway, *Daed's* been hinting for me to find someone. Soon. He's hoping for more *enkelkinder* before he gets too old to enjoy them."

"Do you want more *youngies*?"

"*Ja.* I do." He did. Very much so.

Amity's gaze deepened with warmth and compassion. "Then we'll have to start getting you out and about."

Ethan blew out a breath. Between running the *kaffeeshop*, managing his household and trying to keep his *familie* together, he barely had a minute to spare. The only real break he enjoyed was on Sunday. Three hours in the pews was a welcome respite. He enjoyed the preaching but never stayed to socialize afterward. "I wouldn't know where to begin."

"Come to Rebecca's wedding." Leaning closer, she rested a hand on the bench between them. "Everyone in the community will be there. You should, too."

Ethan blinked. Saying *nein* and dragging his heels weren't acceptable any longer. He felt a presence, as if someone was guiding him gently forward, encouraging him to embrace life once more.

"*Ja,*" he agreed. "We'll come."

Chapter Nine

"Oh, Rebecca, you look lovely."

Smoothing her wedding dress into place, Rebecca beamed. The turquoise shade looked amazing, accentuating her lightly tanned skin. The color also set off her wide green eyes, bringing out the flecks of gold in her irises.

"I can't believe the day is here," she said with a wide smile. "In another hour, I'll be a married woman."

"Time has just flown by," Smiling, Amity helped her sister slip into her stiff white apron. She pulled the back together, then hooked the tabs that kept the apron closed and in place. Made to precise measurements, every fold fell perfectly around her slender figure. "Why it feels like it was just yesterday Caleb got baptized and proposed."

"It's been the longest six months of my life." Suddenly nervous, Rebecca wrung her hands. "I pray Caleb doesn't regret marrying a barren woman."

Bent over the bed, Gail gave a sharp glance. "Hush! You know Caleb doesn't feel that way at all." Working with deft hands, she attempted to dress her toddler in a gown and pinafore.

Jessica kicked her plump little legs in protest. "No-o-o-o, Mama!" Fussy and out of sorts, the *youngie* howled with displeasure.

Rebecca's smile wavered. "He said it doesn't matter—" glancing down, she pressed her hands against her flat stomach "—but I'm hoping treatment for my condition will allow us to have our own."

"I'm praying *Gott* gives you a complete healing from your endometriosis." Done with her chore, Gail scooped up her toddler. "She's teething. Another broke through last night and she's been miserable." Pressing Jessica to her shoulder, she patted her back rhythmically.

"Gah!" Shoving a fist into her mouth, Jessica gnawed at her fingers for relief. A thin line of saliva drizzled down her chin.

Splayed in a nearby chair, Florene wrinkled her nose. "I don't know why you'd want any," she declared in a loud voice. "All babies do is cry and demand attention. A modern woman shouldn't have to put up with these things." Clad in an *Englisch*-style dress and heels, kinky bleached blonde hair covered her shoulders in a cascade. She'd made up her face, going heavy on eye shadow, blush and lipstick.

Amity stiffened. Once again, their youngest sister had decided to reject her Amish upbringing. She rarely missed a chance to criticize or cut down the customs she perceived to be archaic and inferior. Her attitude had led to more than one disagreement. Everyone was tired of arguing. "What a terrible thing to say!" she admonished. "I guess you've forgotten you were little at one time, too."

Twirling a curl around her finger, Florene rolled her eyes. "I didn't ask to be born."

"No, you didn't. But here you are—always bringing your gloomy thunderclouds to block someone else's sunshine." Perturbed with her younger sister, Amity pressed her mouth flat. It took every ounce of self-control she possessed to keep her temper in check. *Someone needs to put some sense in the silly girl's head.*

Caught in the grip of rebellion, Florene hadn't realized how destructive it was to herself and her *familie*. The Bible warned that such an action was a sin and that the disobedient would walk in a parched land. *Gott* would have to deal with Florene. No one else could.

"It's true *kinder* are hard work," Gail declared, holding her little one close. "But they are a gift from the Lord."

"It's not a sin not to have them." Florene eyed Gail's thickening waist. "I don't intend to be tied down with a *haus voll* of crying babes."

Instead of taking offense, Gail returned a sympathetic smile. "No one's forcing you to do anything you aren't happy with," she said softly. "If you don't like being Amish, then don't be. But don't criticize those who embrace and honor the traditions of our church and community."

Florene stood. The chiffon dress she wore was cut well above her knees, giving a scandalous view of her bare legs. Her arms, too, were uncovered. It was inappropriate for an Amish wedding, but she'd insisted on wearing it.

"Whatever." Muttering something under her breath, she stalked toward the door. "I'm done with this argument. I'll live my life as I see fit." Throwing up a hand, she waved her fingers before disappearing.

Visibly trembling, Rebecca blinked back tears. "Why does she have to criticize us all the time? Right now, I feel like everything I've ever wanted in my life is stupid and old-fashioned."

"Pay her no mind, *liebling*," Amity said, attempting to soothe her sister's addled nerves.

Rebecca unexpectedly crumbled, blinking back tears. "I

don't want to do this." She tugged at her apron, attempting to pull it off. "I can't give Caleb the *kinder* he wants."

"Now, stop it!" Amity caught Rebecca's hands before she tore through the clasps. "I've heard Caleb say time and time again that it doesn't matter to him. Love is what makes a *familie*."

Rebecca sniffed. "What if he changes his mind?"

"He won't," Amity said, tightening her grip. "That man is standing outside, dressed in his Sunday best, patiently waiting to marry you. He gave up everything *Englisch* to be with you. Because he loves you."

"And you love him," Gail reminded her. "You told me yourself you fell for him the day he helped deliver Mary Reese's *boppli*."

Rebecca stopped struggling. *"Ja,"* she admitted. "When we were fostering little Matthew, it felt like we were a *familie*. Caleb was so *gut* with him."

"When *Gott* sent Caleb, He truly answered the prayers of so many people," Gail said. "The Bible says the Lord will perform extraordinary miracles. When He brought Caleb to Burr Oak, it was clear He intended to return him to his rightful place in our community. After witnessing that with your own eyes, how could you doubt there won't be more blessings to come?"

"You're right." Rebecca heaved a sigh. "I'm always letting doubt get the better of me. I wish I was as strong in the faith as you and Amity are."

"You are strong. You will make a wonderful *ehefrau* and *mutter* and Caleb will be beside you every step of the way. So will we."

"I just wish I knew what's gotten into Florene. She was doing so well. Going to church and attending the women's Bible study at the community center."

Gail's expression grew shadowed. "I didn't want to say anything because I knew it would upset you."

Rebecca stiffened. "What?"

"She's seeing Zane again," Gail blurted.

Amity's insides twisted into knots. What was Florene thinking? Dating a man with a track record of abuse wasn't a wise idea. Not at all. Zane was a predator. He relied on his father's leverage to get away with his shenanigans, many of them illegal.

"I'd hoped she'd learned her lesson after he got rough with her."

Gail shook her head. "I guess not," she said, struggling to keep her composure. "Levi told me a couple of the hands saw her in town last week. She was in his car, and they were—" A blush crept into her face. "Intimate."

Rebecca's mouth went into a flat line. "What can we do?"

Gail looked between them. "I didn't want to say anything, but Levi has decided to ask Florene to leave the ranch. He doesn't want trouble. If Florene insists on being with Zane, she will have to move out. We can't tolerate any more division in this *haus*."

"It's exactly what the Bible says to do," Rebecca agreed. "If a person stirs up division, we are to have nothing more to do with them."

Stomach clenching tighter, Amity pursed her lips. After her boyfriend had abused her, everyone prayed Florene would learn her lesson and stay away from the *Englisch* world. Instead, she was walking right back into the spider's web. Picturing the two of them together was almost physically painful.

"But is it the right thing to do?"

Jessica began to wriggle in her *mamm's* arms. "Ugh, Mama…"

Gail lowered the little girl, holding her arms as the toddler attempted to balance on her tiny feet. "We're not throwing Florene to the wolves. Levi will give her a chance to cut all ties with him."

"And if she refuses?"

Gail gave them each a long look. "Today's not the time to deal with it. Later, we'll all sit down and hash it out."

The door opened. Elsbeth Hilty stuck her head in. "Rebecca, are you ready?" Serving as an attendant, Elsbeth was directing the arrangements as guests arrived.

Rebecca kneaded her hands together. "Almost," she said, attempting to put on a happy face. "I just need to put up my hair."

Elsbeth nodded. "Do hurry. Bishop Harrison's here and everyone's in place."

"How's Caleb?"

"I've never seen a happier man."

"I keep pinching myself, thinking it's all a dream."

"It's happening, honey," Elsbeth chuckled.

"I'll let everyone know you'll need a few more minutes." Swinging Jessica to her hip with a grace born of practice, Gail headed downstairs.

Rebecca immediately ran her hands through her long hair. "Oh, my. How do I handle this mess?"

Amity reached for a brush. "Sit down. I'll do your hair."

Rebecca sat. "*Danke.* My hands are shaking too hard to handle it."

"I'll make it look nice," Amity said as she moved to stand behind Rebecca's chair. Brushing out the tangles, she pinned the thick strands into a neat bun. A starched white prayer *kapp* finished the simple style. "Done."

Rebecca rose, giving the mirror a fretful glance. Stray locks brushed her nape, accentuating her slender neck. She examined her reflection from every angle. "I'm so pale."

"Give your cheeks a pinch to add some color."

Rebecca obeyed. "How do I look?"

Amity grinned. "I've never seen a prettier bride," she declared, kissing her sister's cheek.

Rebecca smiled. "I hope you're next."

Amity paused, reluctant to admit that probably wasn't going to happen. "I already have so much," she murmured. "It would be selfish to ask for more. I'm content with what the Lord has given me."

Rebecca gave her a long look. "Are you?"

She forced a nod. "I am." Brightening, she added, "I have a new pen pal."

Curious brows rose. "Do you?"

"*Ja.* We're…corresponding. I really like him."

"I'm so happy to hear that." Rebecca reached out and grasped her hands, giving them a little squeeze. "I hope this one works out."

"Today isn't the day to think about me," Amity said, shaking her head. "It's yours." She glanced toward the clock on the bedtable. "And I hate to say it, but you're late."

Rebecca managed a weak smile. "I'm so nervous." Her grip tightened. "I think I'm going to faint."

Amity propped her up. "Oh, no, you don't. You're going to go downstairs and marry that man." She opened the door, then propelled her nervous sibling down the stairs, through the kitchen and out the back door. Guests waited outside, shaded by tents set up in the yard.

All eyes turned as they made their way inside. Everyone was in place, including the groom. Standing with his ministers, Bishop Harrison waited patiently to conduct the religious service.

Handing Rebecca over to the care of her bridesmaids, Amity seated herself on a bench beside Levi. Sammy sat in his lap. To keep him quiet, Gail had given Sammy a cookie. Melted chocolate and crumbs stained his plump cheeks.

Breathing a sigh of relief, she looked around. Familiar faces surrounded her. She'd invited Ethan but had yet to see him. It took a moment to find him in the crowd. Flanked by his *daed* on one side and his *youngies* on the other, he was dressed in his Sunday clothes. Hat in his lap, he'd tamed his unruly curls.

Amity's breath caught. Ethan looked quite handsome. Staring hard, she hardly noticed the nuptials had commenced. As the bishop spoke, Ethan's eyes sparked with memory…and with longing.

He looks so sad. So alone. He needs someone.

Ethan suddenly turned his head. Their gazes collided. They regarded each other in silence. Acknowledging her, he offered a nod. His smile was relaxed. Sincere.

Heart slamming hard, Amity immediately dropped her gaze. Heat crept into her cheeks. Refusing to look a second time, she primly folded her hands in her lap. *No, no, no! Don't look my way!* Hardly daring to breathe, she tried desperately to crush the wayward thought. Where had it come from?

She didn't know.

But it wouldn't go away.

An Amish wedding ceremony was nearly as long as a regular Sunday church service. Through the last three hours, ministers preached lengthy sermons. Hymns were sung, before and after. Most everyone was getting fidgety by the time Bishop Harrison finally ended the ceremony. The happy couple beamed, looking forward to a bright future.

Nuptials over, the celebration was just beginning. An afternoon reception would follow. Thankfully, the weather was mild. The day was clear, but not unseasonably warm. Guests were shaded by the tents and ring of study oaks circling the back lawn. Ice chests stocked with bottled water and other popular beverages were open to anyone needing a cool drink.

Aching to stretch his legs, Ethan waited for the crowd to thin a bit before standing. He'd only met Rebecca once or twice. The groom, not at all. When he had a chance, he'd step up and wish them well.

"Are we staying?" Liam asked.

"Oh, can we?" Charity asked.

"Why not?" *Daed* said, chiming in with his request.

The barrage caught Ethan short. He'd intended to depart right after the ceremony. A glance at the crowd changed his mind. He recognized more faces than he thought he would, both adults and their *youngies*. No one was ready to go home.

He winced. Leaving Oklahoma to move to Burr Oak had already upended their entire lives. They'd lost *familie*, friends and everything familiar. Shoved into a small apartment and put to work in the *kaffeeshop*, no one had the chance to kick up their heels.

That was his fault. One he intended to rectify. Staying would give his *kinder* a chance to socialize with other Amish kids.

"Ja," he said. "We will."

Liam's mouth split into a grin. "Oh, cool. I've been wanting to see the new mustangs Seth told me about. He said they're going to start training them to be cattle horses. Levi said I could help break them in once I got started at the ranch."

Ethan looked at his *sohn*. Since his arrest, Liam had worked hard to rehabilitate himself. Dressed in a white shirt covered by a black vest and matching trousers, the teen had abandoned the buzz cut favored by his *Englisch* friends. The zigzag design was slowly disappearing as his hair grew out. Liam had also followed through on his promise. After paying the repair bill on his bike, he'd given it to Charity. Their move was close to done, and Liam would soon be out on the range herding cattle.

Ethan nodded. "You can." Catching Liam's arm, he added, "But no riding. You're in your *gut* suit and don't need to ruin it."

Liam's head bobbed. "I won't!" Threading his way through the guests, he hurried off to find Seth. The two met up and disappeared toward the corral.

Left standing, Charity gazed longingly at the crowd. Clad in bright frocks, the girls her age chattered and laughed.

Charity glanced down at her plain gray dress. Wrinkling her nose, she crossed her arms and turned away. "They act like babies," she muttered under her breath.

Missing the subtle gesture of self-loathing, Ethan gave her a nudge. "You can't make *freundinnen* if you don't talk to them."

Charity dug in her heels. "I don't want to."

Daed stepped in. "Why don't you go and peek at the rabbits?" He pointed toward the barn and livestock pens. "When we get settled in, we'll build some cages and get our own."

Charity brightened. "Can I?"

Ethan gave up. "I don't see why not."

Happy to be off the hook, Charity skipped away. "I hope we can get some lops," she called back. "A black one. And a white one, too."

Mystified by her behavior, Ethan didn't persist. "I have no idea how to talk to her anymore."

"She's at loose ends," *Daed* said. "She'll do better once school starts."

"September is still weeks away." Less outgoing than her *bruder*, his daughter had fallen into the habits of a loner. Checking out books from the library, she spent hours reading. Afterward, she typed out stories on the old manual type-writer. Tucking the pages in her book bag, she never shared what she'd written with anyone.

"Then find something for her to do."

"Amity mentioned a few activities she might like, like a sewing circle and a book club."

"Capital idea," *Daed* declared. "I concur." Rubbing his chin, he continued. "Don't know if you were paying attention, but there's a work frolic coming up at the church. Both Charity and Liam might enjoy it."

"We will all go," Ethan said, making up his mind.

The conversation dropped to a lull. The bride and groom wove through the crowd, stopping to thank everyone for their attendance. Each guest was given a handkerchief filled with rice and tied with a ribbon as a keepsake, with the wedding date embroidered on the cotton squares. After the reception, the rice would be tossed as a blessing to the couple for a life of prosperity and fruitfulness.

Rebecca greeted them with a smile. "I'm so happy you all came." Lovely in her dress, she glowed with happiness. "I don't believe you've met Caleb," she said and made the introductions.

Ethan held out his hand. "I haven't, but I'm happy to."

Caleb Sutter reciprocated. His grip was sure and firm. "Nice to meet you." Lines at the edges of his eyes and the gray threading his temples marked him as a man nearing forty. Long hair hung in loose curls, his sideburns blending with the beginnings of a beard. Now married, he was expected to grow out his facial hair.

"I've heard you're a doctor of medicine," *Daed* said after his introduction. "I'm curious. How did that come about?"

Taking no offense, Caleb laughed. "I was raised in the *Englisch* world."

Ethan's eyebrows rose. An *Englischer* allowed to marry an Amish girl? He knew the Texas Amish were more permissive than most, but why would Bishop Harrison allow such a union?

Rebecca noticed his confusion. "Caleb's *mamm* was Amish," she explained softly. "She was unwed…"

Ethan nodded. It wasn't unknown for unintended pregnancies to happen during *rumspringa*. At such a time the mistake wasn't to be judged, but quietly taken care of. Even Bishop Swarey acknowledged the fact. He often conducted a hasty union to help the wayward couple avoid scandal.

"She gave me up for adoption," Caleb explained. "It took a while, but *Gott* bought me back where I belonged." His face took on an expression of reflection. "The Lord blessed me with many answers when I came to the faith. I found my purpose, my *familie* and—" he squeezed Rebecca's hand "—my *ehefrau*."

"*Gott* does work miracles," *Daed* agreed, turning his gaze upward. "'Tis my hope Ethan will be so blessed again before I pass."

"You're far from passing, so there's time yet," Ethan mumbled, embarrassed by the declaration. At his age, he wasn't seeking a grand romance. A relationship built on mutual respect would suffice. He didn't expect to fall in love with another woman. But it would be nice if he could tolerate her. "Maybe you should look for yourself," he added, half-jokingly.

"Why, I just might do that." *Daed* grinned as he straightened his suspenders.

Caleb laughed. "My *mamm's* over there if you'd care to meet her." He pointed. Clad in black from head to foot, one woman with silvery hair stood out among the group.

"Don't mind if I do." *Daed* put on his straw hat, angling

it in a manner he perceived to be debonair. "I might be an old rooster, but I've still got a little strut left."

"You look handsome, sir," Rebecca said, offering a wink.

The old man beamed. "I'll take that as a compliment."

The trio departed. The bride and groom linked elbows as they walked. *Daed* grinned, eager to get on with what he called *the business of living.* Open and honest, he never met a stranger. As the Lord commanded, he welcomed all and turned away no one.

Left to himself, Ethan glanced around. When he'd moved to Burr Oak, it hadn't taken long for word to get around that he was a widower. The local matchmaker had visited the *kaffeeshop* a time or two. She'd offered to pair him with several eligible ladies, but he'd declined. If nothing else, the Amish were practical people. After a decent period of mourning, the bereaved was expected to remarry.

Chest taking on a heavy sensation, his throat tightened. The passage of time hadn't made Priscilla's death easier to bear. But life went on. It always did. That's just the way things were.

An elbow jostled him out of his thoughts. "If you've got a hand to lend, we could use it," Levi said. "There are tables to be set up."

"Glad to."

The two men walked to join the others. After the wedding came the feast. Preparing food for over a hundred guests wasn't easy. It took organization and teamwork to seat and serve everyone promptly. Fortunately, the ranch was well-equipped to handle the task. The benches rented for the ceremony were pressed into service a second time, rearranged in front of picnic-style tables for the meal.

Ethan picked up a bench and carried it to its destination. Amity was hard at work, directing the arrangements. The bride and groom would have the place of honor at the reception.

"Put it just there." *Kapp* askew, a few stray curls had escaped. Her quirky smile was bright and cheerful. "We're just about to start serving."

He set the bench in place. "Quite a turnout."

"Rebecca knows just about everyone," she chuckled. "I believe this is the largest crowd we've ever hosted."

"*Danke* for inviting us," Ethan said, glancing through the crowd. "Been a long time since we've enjoyed such a fine day."

She smiled. "I believe I saw Wayne talking to Sarah Bueller. Looks like they hit it off."

"I'd like to see him meet someone. At his age, he deserves to be happy."

"What about you?"

The question caught him by surprise. "I'd like to be."

"But?"

"I don't know if it'll ever happen."

Amity knowingly cocked her head. "You'll never know if you don't open up and reach out."

Looking across the table, Ethan met her gaze. Her wide eyes stayed focused on his. The commotion around them faded away. They both went silent.

His heart sped up, beating in rhythmic thumps. During the ceremony, he'd noticed her noticing him. The exchange of glances had piqued his interest. The spark was there. And it was undeniable. Amity was pretty, sensible and savvy enough to function in the *Englisch* world without compromising her values. And she seemed to like him.

Ask her to walk out.

All he had to do was open his mouth and say the words. But he couldn't. His tongue had turned to stone.

"Amity!" Gail called, waving a hand. "We need extra hands!"

The fragile moment shattered.

Amity blinked, shaking her head. "Excuse me, please." Her lips were parted as if she intended to say more, but she didn't. Offering a nod, she hurried to join the other women toiling in the kitchen.

Ethan heaved a sigh. Amity was gone.

And so was his chance.

Chapter Ten

The thrill of a wedding was followed by a period of getting used to new things. Days passed in the blink of an eye. Everyone knew by now that Gail was expecting a new *boppli*. Levi was overjoyed at becoming a father for the fourth time. Rebecca was adjusting to life as a newlywed. Approved to be foster parents, she and Caleb would soon welcome *youngies* into their home.

The only problem came from Florene, who made no effort to hide her involvement with Zane. Since no one liked him, he wasn't allowed on the ranch. Hoping to talk some sense into her, Gail and Levi planned to hold an intervention. Nobody was excited about it.

Mind tumbling in a hundred different directions, Amity swallowed hard. When the time came, Bishop Harrison had agreed to mediate. Fearing the ultimatum would go badly, she sent up a quick prayer. That was all she could do. Pray and hope *Gott* was listening.

The kettle whistled, jarring her out of her thoughts. Remembering why she'd come into the kitchen, she finished setting up a tray of tea and cookies. Since moving into town, she kept herself busy. Fridays were always her favorite day of the week. Come the evening, members of her sewing circle dropped by to work on their hobbies and discuss the most recent news circulating throughout the community.

Forcing a smile, she greeted her guests. A barrage of questions came from all sides.

"Have you heard from Lew?" Willa Neuhaus asked.

"I must know the latest," Eliza Hochstetler declared.

Leddie Schrag eagerly nodded. "His last letter was so touching." Sighing, she adjusted her glasses to sit higher on her nose.

Amity nodded, filling each cup in its turn. "I've gotten two letters this week." The distraction was welcome. More than just gossiping, the women provided a support system. She cherished being part of such a tight-knit community and couldn't imagine ever leaving it.

"Sounds like he is getting serious." Eliza was a slender, rosy-cheeked woman, and her gaze danced with mischief.

Leddie accepted her cup. "It's all so mysterious. Knowing his box is across from yours must be maddening."

Willa waved a hand, hushing her friend. "Have you caught a glimpse of him?"

Amity shook her head. *"Nee."* Sitting, she added sugar and a splash of cream to her beverage. "We keep different schedules, I'm sure."

Willa ventured a smile. "Has he asked to meet?" Part of a group of Mennonites recently settled in Burr Oak, her friendly nature was magnetic. Only the white scarf covering her fire-red hair set her apart from the other women. Despite the difference, she was welcome.

"Not yet."

"He'd be a fool not to," Leddie said.

"I agree." Gaze sparkling, Willa's nose crinkled. The smattering of freckles on her cheeks and nose gave her an impish look. "Why he'd be missing an unclaimed treasure if he doesn't ask soon."

"You're a nugget of gold for the man who cares to dig deep enough," Eliza said, tittering.

"Someone should give the poor fellow a pickax," Leddie added. Everyone laughed.

Embroidery hoop in hand, Willa attempted to unsnarl a tangle in her thread. "I'm happy to see you happy."

"Do you wonder what he looks like?" Leddie asked.

Eliza bobbed her head. "I imagine him as being tall, with a fine face."

"He probably has broad shoulders," Willa added. "And strong hands."

Amity laughed at their fanciful guesses. Reading through the letters, she'd attempted to picture her unseen friend. But whenever she did, the image that flashed across her mind's screen was cloyingly familiar.

"I always imagine he looks like Ethan," she confessed, half-embarrassed to admit it aloud. It was true. His features were a study in natural perfection, as if *Gott* had crafted him with meticulous care. High cheekbones added a touch of elegance to his humble countenance, and his strong jawline spoke of determination and unwavering resolve. When he smiled, his lips curved with warmth and genuine kindness. He was the epitome of rugged masculinity.

"That fellow who owns the *kaffeeshop*?" Willa asked.

"Aye, I saw him at Rebecca's wedding," Eliza said. "Kept to himself and didn't say much." A social butterfly, Eliza made it her business to know everyone else's business.

"He's a widower, isn't he?" Leddie asked.

"He is," Amity confirmed.

Eliza helped herself to an oatmeal cookie stuffed with

dates and pecans. "Seems to me you've been spending plenty of time helping him," she said between bites.

"*Gott* commands we help others in their need. I could hardly turn a blind eye to a neighbor."

"Your obedience to the Lord's word is admirable," Leddie said. "We should all take heed of your example."

Eliza brushed crumbs off the tips of her fingers. "I don't know if I could have been half so generous. He wasn't welcoming when you moved in."

"That's true. He wasn't. But he did apologize. I am willing to forgive so others will forgive me."

"But nothing more?" Eliza asked.

"*Nein.*" It was true. She liked Ethan. And there was a definite attraction. But his present situation was complicated. She'd be a fool to try to step in. Between his pending move and expanding the *kaffeeshop* online, he barely had a minute to spare. Brief pleasantries were all they'd exchanged.

Willa paused in rethreading her needle. "I think Lew is the fellow you're sweet on." Warmth crept into Amity's cheeks. Her pulse skipped a beat. Exchanging letters with her pen pal had become a special treat. It only took a few days for the mail to travel locally from one box to the other. So far, she'd received quite a few. Each was a delight to read. She memorized every word before tucking the pages in her keepsake box.

Knowing you makes me happy, he'd written. *Your words bring sunshine to my day.*

She waved her hands in denial. "Don't be silly."

Willa grinned. "Oh, I think differently. The moment I said his name, you blushed red as a beet. If that's not love, I don't know what is."

"Amity couldn't possibly be in love with this fellow," Leddie declared sensibly. "She doesn't even know who he is."

Eliza shot her a frown. "Really, Leddie. Don't dash everything with cold water. It's fun to wonder."

"Any clue?" Willa asked.

Amity shook her head. "Lewellyn Christopher or Lewis Coblentz were the first ones I thought of."

"Lewis Coblentz did lose his *ehefrau* a few months ago," Leddie ventured.

"Lewis Senior would be a terrible match," Eliza declared. "He's much too old. And he thinks he hides it, but I know for a fact he tips the bottle."

"What if Lew isn't his real name?" Leddie suggested. "Correct me if I am wrong, but doesn't 'lew' mean 'a place of shelter'?"

"It does," Eliza said, shaking her head. "But what you may not know is that it is also the Hebrew word for *Levite*, or one who is a descendant of Levi, the *sohn* of Jacob and Leah."

Amity nibbled her lower lip. Perhaps Eliza was correct. Maybe Lew C. wasn't a name at all, but had a Biblical or religious significance. *Could it mean a place of shelter in Christ?*

Plausible. But not certain.

One thing was for sure. Through their correspondence, she'd begun to develop feelings for the person behind the letters. It was a treat to immerse herself in the heartfelt exchanges. The words seemed to leap off the pages, carrying a whisper of mystery and a taste of an unknown adventure. Through the pages, they'd formed a deep bond—two souls who had never met but had still managed to form a connection. With each exchange, her feelings bloomed like the first spring blossoms, her soul awakening to feelings she'd never experienced before. The newfound emotion was thrilling.

The bell at her front door buzzed.

"Now, who could that be?" Willa asked.

Shaking off her fanciful thoughts, Amity rose. "I hope you don't mind, but I've invited another to join us." She turned the knob.

Charity stood outside. A flexible wicker basket hung over one arm. "*Datt* said I could come after I finished my chores." She offered a tremulous smile. "I'm not late, am I?"

Amity stepped back, waving her inside with a welcoming gesture. "Not at all. You're right on time." Turning, she addressed the group. "I've invited Charity to join us."

The older women greeted the girl with smiles and introductions.

Taking a seat on the edge of the sofa, Charity folded her hands in her lap. "What am I supposed to do?"

Willa held up her embroidery. "We drink lots of tea, chat and work on our projects." Turning the hoop at an angle, she revealed the scene of a country garden. Every detail was precise, down to the last stitch.

Charity's eyes brightened. "Oh, I wish I knew how to do that."

"It's not hard." Willa glanced toward the girl's basket. "Did you bring something?"

Charity shook her head. "*Nein.* Nothing."

Leddie lifted her knitting, the beginning of a colorful sweater. "We can teach you anything you want to learn."

"Of course, we can," Eliza said, showing off her tatting. To make her living she sold her lace creations to *Englisch* bridal shops. Her custom pieces had adorned many a gown.

"What would you like to try?" Amity asked.

Thinking hard, Charity comically screwed up her face. "*Datt* said we're going to the frolic next weekend. Could I make a dress? Like the girls here wear?"

Amity knew exactly what she meant. While Charity's gray frock reached to her ankles, young *frauleins* in Burr

Oak were permitted to wear a shorter style with the hems cut to midcalf. For modesty's sake, girls over the age of eleven wore leggings or tights to cover their bare skin. A wide variety of colors and patterns was also permissible. Black was reserved for widows and funerals. "That will be your project. We'll all pitch in and help you make a new dress."

"Can I pick the color?"

"Ja." Amity looked at Charity's scuffed boots. She needed new ones. A few pairs of tights wouldn't hurt, either. Once she got the right size, she'd pick up both items. It would help the girl fit in with her Texas peers once she started school.

Deciding to go full steam ahead, Amity didn't anticipate an iceberg might be lurking beneath the depths of her good intentions.

Ethan lay the scissors on the edge of the sink. Leaning over, he brushed away clinging hairs. Straightening, he stared into the mirror. A man with a head of black curls stared back at him. Trimmed and shaped, his beard looked neater, less scraggly.

"A little better," he murmured.

After running a hand under the tap, he dampened his hair to tame his unruly mane. It didn't look bad, as it blended in with his sideburns. The style suited him, softening the edge of his hard jawline and making his face look younger. Only the lines imprinted around the edges of his eyes and corners of his mouth revealed his age and the hardships he'd endured.

Done with his hair, he lifted his suspenders onto his shoulders. His white shirt was neatly pressed, his trousers starched stiff and crisp. He'd darned the holes in his socks and polished his black boots until they shined. After slipping into a vest, he joined the hooks together. A long-sleeved black jacket completed his outfit.

Been a long time since I felt alive.

After Priscilla died, he'd let himself go. Clothes unpressed, teeth unbrushed, body unfed. The very act of breathing was a hardship. His days were gray. His nights were endless. Mind disconnected, he existed in nothingness.

Depression clung for months. He'd withered inside. He wasn't living. He was existing. The pain etched deep into his being, and he'd retreated further into grief. Trapped in his silent anguish, he was unable to function for months. He wandered through each day in a daze, his mind a foggy maze of memories and unanswered prayers. His sole saving grace was his *familie*. Their needs kept him from slipping entirely over the edge.

His return to normalcy was slow and excruciating, but necessary. With prayer and mental discipline, he'd pulled himself out of despair. But the very fact he'd crumbled left a stain on his reputation. Such a person was considered weak, branding him as an outcast. Unstable. Shockingly, his community pushed him to one side. Leaving was the only way to save face.

The move he'd dreaded making was a blessing in disguise. He had a thriving business, a piece of property and hope for a brighter tomorrow.

A heavy hand hammered the bathroom door.

"Datt?" Liam called. "Come on. I need the bathroom."

He started. Was it already near six?

Friday was the beginning of the weekend, a time when working folks could relax. Come five o'clock, most Amish businesses were shuttered, allowing people to take advantage of the long summer evenings. The sun didn't set until close to nine, giving everyone a chance to enjoy a variety of leisurely pursuits. If nothing else, the Amish were a social bunch.

Drawing back his shoulders, Ethan drew in a breath. Tonight would be his first stepping out as a single man. Not only would it give Charity and Liam a chance to hang out with their peers, but they would also learn the value of the community drawing together to support a charitable cause.

Opening the door, he walked into the hall. "It's all yours."

Liam rushed past him to take occupancy. Leaning into the mirror, he grumbled. The bane of every teenager on earth had stuck. Acne.

"*Ach*, my face looks like I've caught the measles." The barest trace of hair also fringed his upper lip. Soon, he'd have enough to start shaving.

Ethan suppressed his chuckle. He'd gone through the same thing when he was a teen. "Don't pick," he warned. "Dab the spots with witch hazel and then use some aloe vera gel. Do it every day. That'll take out the red and help your skin heal."

Liam followed instructions, wiping down his face.

Ethan nodded his approval. Finding a new passion in the rodeo, Liam's attitude had straightened out. He was eager to start working at the ranch.

Satisfied his oldest was on a better path, he walked into the living room. *Daed* sat at the kitchen table. Noah was with him.

"You two look busy."

"Aye, we are," *Daed* said. "I think we've settled on the design for the logo and packaging." Deciding to operate under the Fellowship Kaffeehaus banner, Wayne labored diligently to create his design. His notebook was filled with drawings he felt would reflect the product and its values.

Ethan took a peek. Foregoing the expected horse-and-buggy theme, *Daed* had drawn out a bearded Amish man in a hat. Mug in hand, the faceless figure welcomed all. The pencil drawing was simple but effective.

"I like it," he said.

Noah tapped his pen against a yellow legal pad. "I've put in an order for a few samples to see how it'll look on the packaging. It'll be easy to work into the site design, too."

"Are you sure you want to do this?" he asked. "It's going to be a big project to tackle. And we have yet to get moved."

Daed nodded. "I've spent over forty years learning the craft. Nothing makes me happier than offering folks a hot cup of *kaffee* and a friendly smile. They've come to our place. Now, we'll go to theirs."

Noah grinned. "Shoppers snap up Amish merchandise. They know we put a lot of work and care into our products. It's also a reminder of a simpler time when things weren't so rushed, and people made a real person-to-person connection with those around them."

"And it's nice to sit down and gab over a cup," *Daed* chuckled.

"Yet here we are, rushing to catch up with *Englisch* ways," Ethan commented.

"That's where I come in," Noah said. "I can help you meet your professional goals and creativity while limiting your contact with digital technology. I'm willing to do the work so you can focus on what's important."

Daed backed him up. "I don't think it's any trouble if we use it respectfully and responsibly. I'm willing to pay Noah to do the heavy lifting." The old man might not have understood technology, but he was canny enough to hire those who did.

It was a page straight out of Amity Schroder's playbook. And it looked like it just might be a success. The *kaffehaus* was always busy. Customer requests for the custom blends came in daily. It would be foolish not to take advantage of the opportunity.

"Honestly, if you think about it, adapting to technology

allows Plain folks to lead the lives they are accustomed to," Noah continued.

Ethan eyed the two skeptically. "I don't understand how when it seems we're being pushed out of our world and into theirs."

"Think about it," Noah said. "Any time an Amish business or farm fails, that sends our people out to look for work in the *Englisch* world. That also exposes them to things that aren't appropriate. Things that might lead them away from the church."

"I'd agree that's true."

"By adapting, the Amish can control the narrative we send into the world. The more your *kaffeeshop* grows, the more it offers the community. You don't only make a living for yourself and support your *familie*. You provide jobs, which support our way of living. That strengthens our town and allows us to keep our core values in place."

"It makes sense," *Daed* said. "We're inviting folks to visit us. Not the other way around. Perhaps by seeing how we live, a little bit of it will rub off on them. I'm all for bringing folks to the Lord."

"Amen to anything that saves a lost soul." Ethan glanced at his pocket watch. The hands told him it was close to six thirty. "I'm going to leave you two to your work. It's almost time to go."

Daed rose to refill his cup. "I'm glad you're having an evening out," he said before disappearing into the kitchen.

Ethan left the men to their brainstorming. The conversation had given him a lot to think about. Now, however, wasn't the time. He'd promised Liam and Charity a chance to unwind and have some fun with kids their age. He intended to follow through on his word.

"It's time to go," he called down the hall.

Liam hurried out of the bathroom. "I'm ready." His black trousers were unevenly creased, but neat enough to wear.

"Where's your *schwester*?"

Liam shrugged. "Her room, I guess."

Ethan's gaze moved in the direction of Charity's bedroom. She had yet to come out. Her door was firmly closed.

"Charity?"

The sound of footsteps was followed by a pause. The door swung inward.

Charity stepped out. Coming into the living room, she twirled around gently, the skirt of her dress floating around her like a cloud. A soft shade of pink, the material had a delicate white floral pattern. Her white apron and starched prayer *kapp* were also new, as were the black tights and boots she wore.

"What do you think?"

Ethan's eyes widened. He'd always envisioned his daughter as a symbol of modesty, but this short dress challenged that ideal. The length, or rather the lack thereof, accentuated her legs, exposing more than he deemed appropriate. It was a stark departure from the conservative attire she normally wore.

"Is this the dress Amity helped you make?"

"*Ja*. She helped me pick the material and cut it. But I did all the sewing myself."

"The dress is very nice. But you can't wear it."

Dismay shattered her smile. "Why not?"

"It's indecent, not fit for public."

Charity protested. "It's like the other girls wear."

Ethan cut her off. He believed an Amish woman's clothing should showcase her inner beauty without compromising her dignity. He also worried his *tochter* might invite unwarranted attention or misjudgment from others.

"You aren't other girls. And you won't be wearing it."

Tears welled up in Charity's eyes, threatening to spill over. "But—" Her lower lip quivered, cutting off her words.

Seeing her cry, Ethan's heart melted a little. The unfairness of the situation weighed heavily on her young shoulders. His intentions weren't intended to control or stifle her, but to guide her toward living in ways that aligned with traditional values. That included wearing a dress with a proper hemline.

"Please, don't argue. I've made up my mind."

"You're not being fair," she protested, her voice rising with a mix of anger and desperation.

Ethan pulled in a breath. The dress had a specific reason for being off-limits. "Charity, don't." Crossing his arms, he gave a stern look. "You'll change, or you'll stay home." He was the parent. The last word would be his.

Frustration gave way to a tantrum as Charity's emotions overflowed. Unable to contain the disappointment building up inside her small frame, she stomped her feet. Her face turned red. "I hate you!"

Ethan had no chance to respond.

Dramatically clenching her hands into fists, Charity pushed past him and bolted toward the front door. Throwing it open, her boots carried her swiftly across the threshold. Her clattering steps echoed behind her.

Mind reeling in disbelief, he dashed after her. "Charity, come back here!"

His daughter ignored him. She reached the bottom of the stairs, then wrestled her bike out of its storage place. After jumping on, she pedaled furiously down the alley before disappearing around a corner.

Chapter Eleven

Eyes narrowing in disbelief, Ethan stood motionless. A whirlwind of conflicting feelings buffeted him from all sides. He hadn't expected his *tochter* to throw a tantrum. Normally obedient, she'd pushed back. *Daed* ran up behind him. So did Liam. They'd witnessed the entire argument from beginning to end.

"Looks like Charity got the last word," Liam said, half-breathless.

Ethan scraped a hand across his numb face. What he'd viewed as a minor disagreement had quickly escalated into a fight.

"Aye, she did."

Once again, his home had become a battleground, with harsh words being flung like fiery arrows. The pleasant evening everyone anticipated had fizzled away. No one looked happy.

The door to the neighboring apartment cracked open. "What's going on?" Amity asked. "I heard yelling and running."

Ethan's lips went flat. Looking for someone to blame, he lashed out without thinking. "I fought with Charity," he sputtered. "That dress you helped her make was indecent."

Her door immediately flew open. She stepped outside, a saucy hen ready to peck back. "That is not true!"

"The dress was pink—and cut short enough to expose her legs." Even as he spoke, frustration gnawed at his insides. He didn't stop to question his actions or wonder if he had handled the situation appropriately.

"Did she have on leggings and boots, too?"

He blinked. "I think so."

"That is how every *junges mädchen* in town dresses." To emphasize her point, Amity pointed to herself. "I am wearing the same style now. There's nothing indecent about it."

Chagrin crept in. She was right. There wasn't. Her frock was modest but practical, allowing for freedom of movement.

Argument weakening, Ethan nevertheless persisted. "That style and color is not permitted by our *Ordnung.*" No pattern or other adornment was allowed. The prohibition of bright colors was intended to prevent vanity. The length ensured modesty.

Amity ruffled with offense. "I can't say what the Oklahoma *Leit* permit. But the girls here may choose any color they please. And if they are wearing tights, they may have their dresses shorter for comfort in the summer. The style is perfectly proper here in Burr Oak. The bishop would tell you so himself if he were here now."

Daed looked between the two of them. Wrinkles traced the contours of his face, marking the passage of time and the lessons he'd learned along the way. "Sounds to me like you made much ado about nothing."

His face growing hot, Ethan suddenly felt like a dunce. The Plain way of life had always emphasized unity and respect for tradition. Like his forefathers, he held those principles close to his heart, cherishing the simplicity and harmony they brought to the community. Once again, he'd stumbled over the differences between the Oklahoma and Texas Amish. Charity's last words echoed in his mind, stabbing at his sense of self-worth. His failure to recognize and embrace change had let her down, contributing to the tension between them. The weight of his daughter's pain and resentment settled heavily on his shoulders.

"I guess I overreacted." It was a poor defense, but the only one he had. He blamed himself for not being more patient, and for not understanding the needs of an adolescent girl. He yearned to turn back time, to redo the conversation with newfound wisdom. Instead, he'd messed up everything. Remorse haunted him. The harshness of his words had wounded his daughter.

With a calm and gentle tone, *Daed* responded, "No guessing about it."

Ethan drew in a breath weighed with regret. "How do I mend this?" Sadness mingled with guilt. The profound weight of responsibility was difficult to navigate as a single parent. Every step he took was akin to walking blindfolded through a minefield. He never knew when the next step might lead to an explosion.

Amity was the one to answer. "You say you're sorry."

Chastened, Ethan rubbed his hands across his numb face. "You're right. I owe Charity an apology." He looked toward the direction Charity had taken. "I should go and find her."

"Where is she?" Amity asked.

"She took the bike Liam gave her and left." Ethan spread his hands helplessly. He had no idea where she'd gone.

Worry creased *Daed's* face. "If she's run away, you should call Sheriff Miller."

Amity held up a hand. "I don't think we need to involve Evan. I believe I know where Charity went."

A glimmer of hope found its way into Ethan's troubled mind "If you do, we need to go right away."

"She told me the place she likes best is the library. And

since it's open late on the weekends, I imagine that's exactly where she went."

That made sense. Having the bike gave Charity independence and a sense of responsibility. She was allowed to go to the post office and library without direct supervision. With its panniers and basket, she could easily carry her books and other items.

"It's only a short walk," *Daed* said. "On a bike, she'd be there in a few minutes."

Stepping inside the open door, Ethan reached for his hat. "I'll go now."

"Are we still going to the frolic?" Liam asked.

Ethan nodded. "*Ja.* You can go ahead if you want." There was no reason to ruin the entire evening for everyone. "I'll be there as soon as I find Charity."

"Wait. I'll go with you." A hint of anxiety flickered in Amity's gaze. Her eyes, usually calm and peaceful, held a restless glimmer. Lines of worry subtly etched themselves on her smooth forehead.

"You don't have to," Ethan said, shaking his head. "I made the mess. I'll clean it up."

"I want to." She opened her door, then extended her arm toward the wooden peg where her things were hung. Her fingers curled around a hand-knitted shawl. After plucking it down, she draped it over her shoulders. An essential part of an Amish woman's attire, it shielded her from the evening breeze.

Ethan nodded. "Let's go." Eager to be on his way, he headed down the stairs. Descending to street level, gravel crunched beneath his boots.

Amity followed behind. When she stepped down to join him, the faint scent of her freshly washed clothing wafted through the air. Hair tucked neatly beneath her *kapp*, she looked perfectly prim and proper.

With measured strides, Ethan set off toward the library. His gait was steady and purposeful. Each step carried a sense of intention; the soft thud of his boots on the hard ground matched the steady beat of his heart. The sights and sounds of the town unfolded before him. Come the weekend, the cobbled streets were busier, teeming with people eager to take advantage of the longer summer evenings. Children roamed the park nearby, their laughter filling the air as they played traditional games. Gas-powered vehicles did their best to navigate around horses clomping in front of buggies. Amity kept up the pace, matching him stride for stride.

Ethan glanced at her determined figure. Their argument had passed without leaving a trace. If she held a grudge, she never showed it. Her concern was for Charity, and it touched him deeply.

As he replayed their recent encounters in his mind, he began to see beyond the surface of their disagreements. The glimmer in Amity's eyes when she stood up for her beliefs and the fervor in her voice as she defended her perspective were signs of a spirit that captivated him. Focusing so much on their differences, he'd failed to acknowledge her charming qualities, such as the way she laughed. And the warmth of her smile could melt the iciest manner.

He'd fallen in love with the very essence of who Amity was—her passion, her determination and her unwavering dedication to their shared heritage and faith. The realization hit him with a force he couldn't ignore.

Thankfully, the library came into view.

Forced to refocus, Ethan tucked away his feelings. First, he needed to settle things with Charity. He was the one in the wrong, and he owed her an apology.

A modest structure with large windows, the building's humble exterior was complemented by neatly trimmed bushes and flower beds that add a touch of color to the surroundings. A sign at the entrance proudly carried the name of the library, inviting visitors to step inside. Open to all, it stood as a hub of knowledge and community to *Englisch* and Amish alike.

They walked up the steps and entered. The faint scent of books greeted them. Cozy and intimate, the warm lighting cast a soft glow on the shelves. The sound of hushed whispers created a serene ambiance.

At the center of the library stood a large circulation desk. Staff was available to help patrons with checkouts, returns and inquiries. Several large bulletin boards displayed all the latest community announcements, local events and information about library programs. A bank of desks with computers was open for public use. It wasn't unusual to see Amish folks using the resources for business or online research.

Times have changed.

Bishop Harrison was right. Plain folks had to keep up or be left behind. It wasn't just a matter of common sense. It was a matter of survival. The key to balance was to master modern advances while maintaining Plain traditions and disciplines.

The librarian offered a warm smile as they approached. An *Englischer*, she wore comfortable yet professional attire—a crisp blouse paired with a knee-length skirt. Her long hair was pulled back into a ponytail. A vibrant pink streak was the sole sign of her rebellion. The ID card hanging from a lanyard around her neck identified her by name.

Remembering his hat, Ethan whipped it off. "Excuse me, Miss Pressler. My name is Ethan Zehr. I'm looking for my *youngie*. She comes here a lot to check out books."

The woman brightened. "I remember meeting you a few months ago. You're Charity's father."

"*Ja.* I am."

Miss Pressler smiled warmly. "She came in about twenty minutes ago." She pointed toward a cozy reading area with comfortable armchairs and reading lamps. "She's just there."

"*Danke.*"

"You're welcome. Let me know if you need anything else."

"We'll be fine, Brenda," Amity answered. She gave a knowing look. "Are you ready to talk to her?"

"*Ja.* I think so."

Ethan abandoned the front desk. Aside from a few other patrons, the reading nook was empty.

Amity tugged his sleeve. "There," she said, pointing to the farthest corner.

Ethan visually tracked her gesture. To keep to herself, Charity had chosen a large upright old-fashioned chair with a high back. Her face was red and puffy, betraying traces of tears. Her delicate fingers gently gripped the worn edges of a large picture book, *Alice's Adventures in Wonderland.* Concentrating on her reading, her gaze moved with a dedicated focus across the pages.

At that moment, all his worries and fears evaporated, replaced by an overwhelming sense of gratitude. *Thank You, Gott, for bringing her to this haven.*

Heart pounding with a mix of anxiety and anticipation, he froze. Doubt echoed his troubled thoughts. He'd already messed up once. He didn't want to make the same mistake twice.

"What do I say?"

"Speak from a place of humility," Amity whispered, mindful of their hushed surroundings. "All you have to do is say you're sorry and listen with an open heart. Charity deserves the same considerations you've given Liam. It's not fair to allow him latitude but offer her none." Her words, gently spoken, were wise ones.

Ethan nodded. Despite the fight, his love for his youngest *kinder* burned as brightly as ever, a flame that refused to be extinguished. No matter how intense their disagreements may be, his love for both his *youngies* would endure for the rest of his life.

"You think she will forgive me?"

She placed a reassuring hand on his arm. "The power of forgiveness is a balm for the wounds others inflict. And the love of our *kinder* is a precious gift. It's through the trials of raising them that we learn and grow ourselves. I believe *Gott* gave both of you a lesson today. Charity was too prideful, and you were too judgmental."

Humbled by her wisdom, Ethan bowed his head.

"Danke," he murmured with renewed determination. "I will do better." He knew it would be hard to rebuild the trust that had been shattered. But he was determined to mend the fractures.

With renewed commitment, he prepared to take the first step toward reconciliation. He also made an internal decision. *Daed* was right. He needed a helpmeet.

Desperately.

A work frolic was more than a chance to socialize. It was also a time when folks came together in support of those in need. In this case, the charity was the *Boppli Bank*, created to help single mothers provide for their *youngies*. Handmade blankets and clothes were the most needed. Diapers, bottles, formula and other baby items were also welcomed.

Gathering the donations was one thing. Getting everything ready for distribution was another. Volunteers were needed to sort, fold and package the parcels. Everyone was encouraged to participate. To teach *youngies* the value of providing for those less fortunate, parents brought their *kinder* to help with the busy work. If a *kind* was old enough to walk and talk, they were old enough to lend a hand.

The chatter of merriment filled the air. Laughter and conversation echoed throughout as people shared stories, jokes and warm embraces. Boys and girls worked together under the watchful eyes of their parents, helping create the care packages. Once the task was finished, everyone would partake in the buffet. Enticing the appetite, the aroma of delicious food wafted from the kitchenette.

Caught in the sorting and folding of cloth nappies, Amity barely had a chance to catch her breath. While some mothers didn't mind using disposable diapers, many preferred ones that could be washed and dried for reuse. No woman needing help was turned away. The *Boppli Bank* served Amish and *Englisch* alike.

Though she'd arrived with the Zehr *familie*, everyone had split up. Liam had joined Seth and Levi's group. Pressed into babysitting, Charity helped keep up with a group of toddlers. Chatting with the other girls, her eyes sparkled with enthusiasm. Beaming with pride, she twirled a few times to show off her new dress. Ethan joined a group of men packing the care bundles in cardboard boxes. Tape in hand, he sealed each box before handing it off to the next person.

"There you are!" A set of arms pulled her into a warm embrace.

Laughing, Amity hugged back. "I wondered where you were. I didn't see you when I came in."

"I didn't expect such a turnout tonight." Face glowing with happiness, Rebecca's eyes shined with gratitude. "Donations have been pouring in. I think we'll be stocked for a year—maybe more."

"That's amazing. Congratulations on your hard work."

"All the glory goes to *Gott*," Rebecca said. "It couldn't have happened without the Lord's blessing."

Amity smiled, thinking how wonderful it was to see Rebecca happy. Roped into fostering an abandoned newborn, Rebecca was appalled to discover the lack of services for new mothers. Determined to help, she put her energy into making her venture a success. Partnering with the local health clinic had given her a base of operations. Notable members of the community also served as patrons, donating the funds to cover the administrative fees and other expenses. Bishop Harrison permitted the use of the community center for fundraising and organizing donations. As a physician, Caleb made sure women and their babies stayed healthy.

"Amen to that." She looked around. "I haven't seen Gail anywhere."

"She wasn't feeling well, so she decided to stay home."

"Nothing bad, I hope."

"Just the usual morning sickness," Rebecca said. "Except hers seems to be worse in the evening. Levi's got Seth and Sammy with him so she can rest."

Rebecca shook her head. "I don't guess Florene bothered to come?"

"Of course not. Helping might take her away from running around with Zane." Worry rippled across her expressive face. "I'm worried he's dragging her into something she's too afraid to get out of."

"I'd hoped when they broke up that Florene would have the sense to stay away from him," Amity commented.

"Caleb tried to talk to her again, but she brushed him off." Rebecca swallowed hard, trying to keep her emotions from overwhelming her. "I wish she'd find an Amish man. Someone who could make her forget Zane ever existed."

"That would be the best thing for her."

Rebecca pressed out a heavy sigh. "As it is I think everyone's sick of the entire matter."

"Are we still going to meet Sunday after church?" Amity asked.

"Ja."

"I'll be there."

Overwhelmed by emotion, Rebecca began to choke up. "I hope we can talk some sense into her before something bad happens."

Amity caught her hands, offering a squeeze of reassurance. "I'll pray the Lord steps in and leads her back to the church."

"We all are." Taking a moment to compose herself, Rebecca offered a smile. "But enough about that trouble. How are you? I haven't had a chance to visit with you since the wedding."

Amity had no chance to answer. A group of women approached, waving to catch Rebecca's attention.

"Everything is sorted, packed and ready for distribution," Lottie Beeman said, smiling broadly.

"We've got almost a hundred boxes," another chimed in.

"We thought you might want to say a few words to everyone before we grab a bite to eat," a third woman urged.

Drawn away by her friends, Rebecca disappeared into the group. She gave a quick look back, mouthing a few unintelligible words. And then she was gone, back to the task of overseeing her foundation.

Amity watched her go. *Left on my own again.*

She sighed. That's the way it always was. Despite knowing everybody in town, at the end of the evening, she was always the one left standing alone.

Now that the work was done, people were ready to relax.

A buffet was set up, allowing everyone to serve themselves. The women volunteering to do the cooking began to bring out the food. As it wasn't a formal sit-down meal, a variety of easy-to-handle finger foods was served. Accompanying the traditional sandwiches were deviled eggs, fried mac-and-cheese balls and at least a dozen other tasty selections. Dessert was chocolate or vanilla ice cream, served in waffle cones.

"May I join you?"

Amity glanced up. Ethan stood with two drinks in his hands. "You looked thirsty," he said, offering one of the plastic cups. "I hope you like lemonade."

She accepted the offer. "I do."

"I wasn't sure." He nodded toward the drinks station. "The selection is kind of limited. It's iced tea, lemonade or water."

"Danke." She caught the end of the straw and took a sip. The tart-sweet drink hit the spot.

"Would you like something to eat?"

She declined the offer. "I'm fine. Now that the work's done, I was just about to head home."

Disappointment dimmed his gaze. "I was hoping you'd sit with me." Clearing his throat, he added, "If you don't mind."

Amity looked at him with a mix of surprise and curiosity. Though they'd smoothed things over earlier in the evening, he'd hardly said two words to her since then. "I can stay a little longer."

"Why don't we sit there." He indicated a quiet corner away from the noisy group. A few tables and chairs filled the space.

"All right."

They sat, maintaining a respectful distance, yet close enough to engage in conversation.

Ethan leaned forward. Setting his elbows on the table, he

clasped his hands together, revealing the nervousness that gripped him. "I just wanted to say I'm sorry for blaming you for Charity's dress."

Amity took his apology in stride. "You are her *vater*. And you aren't accustomed to seeing her in clothes of that cut and color. If it means anything, I did want her to show you the material before we made the dress. But she wanted to surprise you."

"It's not that. I suddenly realized she's growing up."

"*Youngies* do tend to do that."

"You don't understand. From the day she was born, Charity has been a joy. I remember holding her in my arms, her tiny fingers clutching on to mine, and her innocent eyes gazing up at me—" Emotion suddenly tightened its grip, throttling his words. "Anyway, it struck me then that my *kleines mädchen* is a young *fraulein* now. She's starting to notice the *bois*…and they're noticing her. I can't say I'm ready for it."

Ethan's confession touched Amity deeply. Anyone with two eyes could see his grief was still a raw, open wound. The overwhelming sense of emptiness and loss he felt was etched in the lines around his eyes and mouth.

"I'm glad to help any way I can."

"I know. I'm grateful." Drawing a breath, he pulled back his shoulders. "Tonight showed me I need a helpmeet with a *gut* head on her shoulders to help finish raising my *youngies*. A woman like you."

Her jaw dropped. The timbre of his voice thrummed her senses. "Ethan, are you…?"

He nodded. "You've said you'd like to get married, but no one's asked. Well, I'm asking." Pausing, he cleared his throat. "I know it's sudden, but I am serious. I want you to be my *ehefrau*."

Pure shock filled her. The very air around her grew heavy,

charged with the weight of his unspoken expectations. Caught off guard, her mind raced like a wild horse on an uncharted path. She'd always dreamed of a romantic proposal.

This wasn't it.

Lowering her head, she stared at the bare tabletop. A volley of confusing emotions battered her from all sides. She'd never admit it out loud, but she had already given Ethan due consideration. Many times. He was a decent *Gottesfurcht* man. And a hard worker. She liked the way his blue eyes sparkled when he spoke. And the way his warm smile widened, and his laughter echoed in her ears when he was happy. At such times, her heart fluttered with desire. She sometimes even dreamed of them sitting together, holding hands, as they discussed a future together.

And then there were times like tonight, when reality set in. She couldn't imagine being with a man who picked apart every detail or questioned every decision she made. Ethan made mountains out of molehills time and time again. True, he always apologized. But he was deeply conservative. She was modern and progressive. The two didn't mesh well. They were just too different. They shared ownership in the same building.

And nothing else.

The silence stretched on. Uncomfortable became unbearable. A dash of cold water in the face would have been more welcome.

"I take it your answer is *nein*?"

She glanced up. "It is."

"I could give you a *gut* life," he said. "You would want for nothing."

"I have that now."

His eyes narrowed. "Is it that fella you've been writing?"

The question sent a spray of goose bumps across her bare

arms. Her heart had already embarked on a flight of fancy, one she had not yet spoken aloud. It was a journey marked by an infatuation she dared not utter, for it belonged to another—a mysterious correspondent who haunted her like a sweet melody.

"I am involved with someone else," she confirmed. "But that's beside the point."

"Meaning?"

"I don't think you're ready to remarry. Not me. Or anyone else." Though she believed her presence had brought him some comfort, she couldn't shake the feeling Ethan still pined for the woman he'd deeply cherished. The notion weighed heavily on her; she didn't want to be a mere replacement, a stand-in. He asked out of need. Not from any real affection.

Ethan's shoulders visibly sagged. "I've had the love of my life," he admitted, dragging a hand across his bearded face. "It would be selfish to hope for that gift a second time."

"It's not that you don't deserve to be happy in a second marriage. It's that I deserve not to be a convenience or an easy solution to your problems. If you need a nanny, hire one. But I'm not interested in the position, thank you very much."

Discomfort clouded Ethan's expression. "*Danke* for your honesty. I appreciate it." He pushed his hands against the table and rose to his feet. "I think I should go." Politely excusing himself, he walked away.

Amity watched him leave. The air around her seemed heavy, mirroring the tension she felt inside. The finality of her decision gnawed like a starved animal.

A stray tear trickled down her cheek, but she didn't call out. Nor did she go after him. She believed she'd made the right choice.

But it didn't ease the deep ache of regret.

Chapter Twelve

Florene stood in the middle of the living room. She wore ripped jeans and a T-shirt, a stark reminder of her departure from traditional Amish ways. Arms crossed, she glared through narrow eyes. Tension crackled around her.

"I don't like being attacked like this," she said, flinging out the words. "You're all against me."

Equally upset, everyone stared back. Gail and Levi. Rebecca and Caleb. Bishop Harrison was also in attendance, overseeing things with a calm and level presence. His stern expression reflected the weight of responsibility he bore as he listened to the argument unfold. To spare the *youngies*, Gail had Ezra and Ruth Weaver keeping an eye on them.

Hesitating to immerse herself in the tempestuous conflict, Amity sat quietly in her place. Her heart longed for unity, a peaceful resolution that would bridge the divide between her loved ones. *Lord, please let this go well*, she silently prayed. *Let us settle the matter with love and understanding, not with bitter words.*

Bishop Harrison broke the impasse. "Florene, we have gathered here tonight to address the path you have chosen to walk," he began, his words carrying a sense of sorrow. "Your *familie* has long embraced the Amish way of life—

but you have turned away from our teachings, our customs and our faith."

Florene's gaze shifted, defiance unfurling in her expression. "I prefer *Englisch* ways, Bishop," she said, refusing to temper her anger. "And it's also true I may do so. I am not baptized and have made no vow to *Gott* or the church. Nor do I have any intention of doing so."

"As much as it pains me, you speak the truth," the bishop agreed. "You are free to choose your path. But I would caution you to think long and hard before you do. Once you have walked away, there may be no coming back."

Gail was the first to add a plea. "Florene, please understand we want you to stay. But unless you agree to stop seeing Zane, that's not going to be possible."

Levi chimed in with his concerns. "Just because he says he loves you today, doesn't mean he won't mistreat you tomorrow."

"He's been physical with you before," Caleb reminded her. "Any man who lays hands on a woman isn't to be trusted. Forgiven, *ja*. But trusted? *Nein*."

"Don't you understand Zane is bad news?" Rebecca trembled as she spoke, prompting Caleb to place a protective arm around her shoulders.

Florene's face hardened as she listened to everyone. Ignoring all, she turned to Amity. "You've been quiet, Miss Goody Two-shoes," she said. "Isn't it your turn to attack me?"

Refusing to be baited, Amity shook her head. She prided herself on being a peacemaker and avoiding conflict whenever possible. "I believe you have the right to make your own choices. But I also believe Gail and Levi have the right to consider the sanctity of their home."

"It's my home, too! They haven't got any right to force me out because I want to live a different way."

Levi stood to face her. "Not when your actions create discord among us."

"The Lord says we are to avoid those who bring trouble," Rebecca said, backing him up. "If a person sows division, we are to warn them. If they refuse, we are to send them away."

Florene smirked. "How convenient you're all forgetting what the Bible says about forgiveness and kindness."

The argument escalated. Voices grew louder and more passionate. Piercing accusations reverberated throughout the room.

Bishop Harrison raised his hands to tame the heated atmosphere. His calm presence radiated with authority. "I have heard enough," he announced, addressing the group. "If you can't render a decision among yourselves, I will make the judgment for you."

The room fell into an uneasy silence as everyone exchanged glances.

Holding their attention, the church elder continued, "As long as there is division among you, there will be no peace."

"It's nothing I want in this *haus*," Levi said, shaking his head. "Zane has a bad reputation, and we all know it. We don't welcome that here."

"Perfectly understandable," the bishop said. "I happen to know the person in question, and I agree."

"Zane's changed. He promised he wouldn't—"

Caleb stepped up, cutting her off. "Wouldn't what? Hit you?"

"Zane was mad," Florene retorted. "He thought I was cheating on him. And he didn't hit me."

Caleb snorted. "He just shook you so hard that you had bruises all over your arms. That makes everything okay." Frustrated, he ran his hands through his hair. "If only you could see what I did when I was working in emergency medicine."

Rebecca rested a calming hand on his arm. "Now, dear, let's not go there. It's too upsetting for you."

"My relationship with Zane is complicated." Snared in a web spun by Zane's manipulative ways, Florene continued to defend him. By the look on her face, she longed to believe change was possible. "I've had enough of your self-serving, sanctimonious simpering. You all speak of forgiveness, but you won't give Zane a chance to redeem himself."

The outburst stunned everyone. Even Bishop Harrison looked disturbed.

Amity felt a chill clutch her insides. Tears welled up in her eyes. Florene had gone too far. The traditions and the expectations of their community loomed like an insurmountable wall between them.

Levi took the hard line. "For the well-being of this *familie*, we can no longer tolerate your choices." He exchanged a sorrowful glance with Gail before continuing. Her nod of approval prompted him to a stark conclusion. "If you want to be with Zane, you can't live here."

"You'll have to move out," Gail echoed.

"That's not fair! I love Zane and he loves me."

Gaze filled with disappointment, the bishop's voice was unwavering. "My child, we have all tried to guide you, but it seems you are determined to have your way. A *haus* divided cannot stand."

"Then I'll leave!" Defiance darkened Florene's face. "I'm packing right now!" Breaking into a run, she dashed up the stairs. Her bedroom door slammed shut.

Silence followed her departure.

Gail's tear-streaked face reflected her anguish. "I should go and talk to her."

Levi held her back. *"Nein.* She's made her decision."

"It pains me to see her blinded to the truth," Bishop Harrison commented, shaking his head with regret.

"The more we speak against Zane, the more she wants to be with him," Rebecca said. "It's like she's mesmerized by the idea of forbidden love."

"I've seen it a thousand times before," Caleb said. "She's convinced her love will make him a better man. She's mistaken his jealousy for affection, believing he cares about her. All it does is give him more control."

"Why can't she see that?" Levi demanded.

"Because men like Zane know how to be charming. And they are. At first. She doesn't realize it, but Zane is preying on her emotions, making it all about how he feels—how badly she hurt him and things like that. She'll do her best to please him. Before she realizes it, she'll be trapped."

Fright widened Gail's eyes. Her face was a pale oval of fear. "We can't let Florene keep seeing a man like that."

"We can't stop her," Levi said quietly. "She's of age."

Gail glanced toward the staircase leading to the second floor. Above their heads, Florene stomped through her room. "Do you think she'll have a change of heart when she cools down?"

Levi reached for her hand, offering a reassuring squeeze. "I don't know, honey. All we can do is wait and see."

A buzz interrupted.

"Sorry, my pager," Caleb explained, checking the message. "Looks like I'm needed at the clinic."

"On a Sunday?"

"People get sick twenty-four-seven. Dr. Wiley can't handle everything himself."

"There's always an emergency," Rebecca explained, gathering her shawl and knitted handbag. Bidding the bishop and the rest of the *familie* goodbye, the couple departed.

"I need to check the cattle pens." Levi reached for his hat as he headed toward the back door. "Couple of fences went down. Need to make sure the hands got the barbed wire re-strung."

Gail momentarily pursed her lips. Fatigue and worry darkened the circles under her eyes. "I should go pick up Sammy and Jessica. Ruth's had them long enough. She shouldn't have to spend her day off babysitting."

Bishop Harrison stepped up. "If you like, I will speak to Florene in private."

Gail gave him a grateful look. "*Danke*, Bishop. Maybe you can talk some sense into her." Pausing, she straightened her *kapp* in preparation to go out. "Amity, please get the bishop a cup of tea."

Amity nodded. "Of course." Rising from her place, she hurried into the kitchen.

"*Danke,*" Clark Harrison said, taking a seat at the long kitchen table. "I'll wait a few minutes before I go upstairs."

A kettle simmered atop the wood-burning stove. Filling a metal ball from a canister of loose tea leaves, Amity dropped it in the water to steep. Minutes later, she delivered two steaming cups.

Bishop Harrison added a dollop of cream. Stirring, he gave her a close look. "While I've got a moment to sit, I'd like to speak with you about a matter that has come to my attention this morning."

Amity felt her blood pressure drop. She couldn't imagine what anyone would have to complain about. "Have I done something wrong?"

"Of course not." The bishop shook his head. "Wayne Zehr

approached me after church this morning. He said Ethan asked you to marry him, but you said no."

Hands trembling, Amity lowered her cup. Believing her dilemma with Ethan to be solved, she didn't see any reason to revisit the subject. He'd asked her to be his wife. She'd declined. Case closed. She'd only caught a brief glimpse of him at church. He'd given her a polite nod…and nothing else. His expression was pleasant, masking what he might have felt inside.

"Ethan did ask," she confirmed.

"But you weren't compelled to accept?"

Mouth going dry, she shook her head.

"May I ask why?"

Amity stared at him, struggling to find an answer. She prayed the ground would open and swallow her up, but it didn't happen. "We h-hardly know each other," she stammered after a moment's silence. "And we argue. A lot." Regaining her composure, suspicion crept in. "Did he ask you to talk to me? To change my mind?"

The bishop held up his hands. "I simply wanted to get both sides. Far be it from me to press if you aren't willing."

Amity crossed her arms. "Well, I'm not."

Bishop Harrison angled his head. "You are almost twenty-six. Your chances to wed are…um, slender."

"That's not true. I have prospects. I have a pen pal, and we're quite involved."

The bishop folded his hands and placed them on the table-top. "Close enough to be engaged? Promised to each other?"

Chagrin suffused her. "We've only ever written letters."

The bishop's eyebrows rose. "You've not met this fellow in person?"

"Nein." Embarrassment scorched her cheeks. "You must think I'm a fool."

Gray-haired and wise, Bishop Harrison returned a somber look. "I'd advise you to rethink the man standing in front of you, asking for your hand, over one who hides behind a veil of paper and ink."

His remark drew the breath from Amity's lungs, forcing her to grapple with her emotions, her faith and her duty. Tension knotted her nerves. Torn between the values instilled in her from birth and the yearnings that stirred within her, the weight of uncertainty was a heavy burden.

Tears suddenly blurred her vision. She began to tremble.

Had she tossed away the sensible choice to follow a flight of fancy?

"I can't believe we're back in a *haus* of our own," *Daed* said.

Stepping out of the van he'd hired for the afternoon, Ethan eyed the huge truck accompanying them on their journey. Apartment emptied, the moving van held all their worldly goods. Deal finalized, funds transferred, the Klatch property formally changed hands. The rambling old *haus* stood empty, ready to welcome a new *familie*. The barn awaited the arrival of horses and other livestock. A clutch of stray cats skittered right and left, panicked by the commotion.

"It was a long wait," he agreed. "But we finally made it."

Pulling in a breath of fresh country air, Ethan's gaze swept over the sprawling landscape. The day was warm and clear, edged with heat but not unbearable. A few clouds drifted across the wide blue space. Thankfully, a storm wasn't in the forecast.

It's a fine day to start again.

"Come on," *Daed* said, waving a happy hand. "We'll pick our rooms and start moving our things."

Charity and Liam hopped out and raced up the front steps.

Shaded by the verandah, the door was propped open, ready to greet the new occupants. Their joyous laughter rang out as they explored the empty rooms. Bare floors beckoned throughout, ready to be adorned with hand-woven rugs. The memory of past times faded away, soon to be replaced with those created by the new occupants.

Walking at a slower pace, Ethan stepped under the threshold. With each step, a profound sense of gratitude and responsibility filled him. His heart swelled with pride as he gazed at the sturdy walls that would shelter his loved ones. The walls around him were a sanctuary, a refuge where his *youngies* would grow and flourish. It also marked a step toward the future, where his *kinder* could begin to forge their paths.

Everyone went through the house, exploring its many features. Empty, it appeared much larger. Along with the kitchen and central living room, there were five bedrooms, a laundry room and a modern bathroom. There was also a side room with a large open hearth. It was far more space than they needed, but every inch was welcome. No more bumping elbows, as they had in the cramped apartment in town. There was plenty of space to grow. Two more *youngies* would easily fit in. Maybe even three.

A sigh winnowed past his lips. Ready to embrace this new life, he yearned for a companion to share his days, and more *kinder* to fill his arms.

But the woman he'd chosen had turned him down.

The days had flown by since the disastrous encounter. One week had passed, and then another. However, their friendship wasn't the same. Save for a fleeting nod or a brief greeting, they rarely spoke. Avoiding the common entrance, each stayed to their respective side. If they did converse, the subject usually concerned the property or its utilities. If he'd possessed the funds, he would have offered to buy her out, lock, stock and barrel.

Moving day was, frankly, a relief. It put some distance between them. They were no longer close neighbors, in town or the country. The ranch Amity's *familie* owned was miles down the road. New renters would soon occupy the vacant apartment in town.

Through it all, he'd learned a lesson. Sometimes an unanswered prayer was the answer. It wasn't because *Gott* didn't care or wasn't listening. It was because his desire was selfish. Concerned about his own needs, he hadn't given Amity's feelings any consideration. He assumed a woman of a certain age would be eager to wed. Grateful, even. That wasn't the case.

Ethan recalled the day he'd summoned the courage to approach Amity. He couldn't blame her for saying no. His proposal was clumsy and lacking in emotion. Admiring her common sense and unwavering devotion to the faith, he believed they could create a comfortable and beneficial partnership. Afraid to confess his true feelings, he yearned for a tender touch to mend the cracks in his heart.

The look on Amity's face warned him he'd blown his chance the moment the words tripped over his tongue. But it was too late to do the day over. Respecting her decision didn't ease the ache inside. His soul remained burdened with unrequited longing.

The chatter of happy voices drew him back to the present.

Tucking his thoughts away, Ethan looked on as Charity and Liam scurried about. Their youthful energy and laughter was contagious. The movers, too, began the arduous task of unloading the truck. Hired for the afternoon, the men were determined to be done before sundown.

Daed directed the workmen, pointing out where he

wanted things to go. He immediately homed in on the extra side room, which had once been part of the kitchen. "I'm setting up my grinders and roaster here," he declared. An enormous piece of equipment, the cast-iron *kaffee* roaster he used was over a century old. His wood and brass grinders were also antiques. "Plenty of space to set things up just the way I want."

"Dibs on this room!" Liam called from down a long hall.

Charity tentatively opened a door directly across. Her gasp filled the air. "There's a desk and a chair."

Ethan joined her. The room faced the east, with a wide window that allowed plenty of sunlight to stream in. Cleaned from top to bottom after Jenna and Giles Klatch moved out, the elderly couple decided to leave heavier pieces of furniture behind. Their new place didn't have the space. Nor did it make sense to put the items in storage. Whatever was left behind, Giles promised, would belong to the new owners.

"Is this the room you want?"

Charity nodded. "*Ja.* I do."

"Then it shall be yours." Ethan gave his youngest a nudge, urging her to explore.

Entering, Charity eagerly ran a hand over the surface of the old desk. Crafted with skill by an Amish carpenter, the piece embodied simplicity and elegance. Hewn from sturdy oak, its surface bore the marks of flickering candles and inkwells that once graced its surface. Beside it, the chair stood ready, awaiting a new occupant. High-backed and rigid, a much-needed cushion would make it more comfortable to sit.

"Can I have them?" The question danced in her eyes. "For my writing?"

"They're all yours."

Grinning from ear to ear, she rushed to hug him. "I can't

wait to set up *Poppi's* typewriter. My lamp and books will look nice, too."

"It's your room," he said. "Decorate it how you wish."

As he often suffered insomnia, Ethan chose the one nearest the kitchen and back door. By happenstance, it was also the largest. But that wasn't why he wanted it. During the times he was unable to sleep, he liked to slip out and wrap himself in the soft velvety folds of night. The quiet soothed his shattered nerves, allowing him the peace to think, and to pray. Able to come and go as he pleased, his restless wanderings wouldn't disturb those who were able to find peace in slumber.

Satisfied with his choice, he wove his way around displaced furniture and boxes packed to the brim with household possessions. Belonging to a bygone era, the walls pleaded for a fresh coat of paint. Warped floorboards creaked underfoot. In the kitchen, a thin layer of soot clung to the stone around the wood-burning stove.

Ethan paused to trace a patch of faded paint. He looked forward to making the repairs and redecorating. It would be his odyssey; every swing of the hammer, every stroke of his saw, would resonate with purpose. Through the discipline of hard work, he hoped to renew his flagging spirit.

With most of the heavy furniture in place, the workmen began to unload items at the back of the trailer. The cardboard boxes were packed to the brim. Aware the day was getting away, Ethan walked outside to help. *Daed*, Charity and Liam were already sorting through the disarray. Working in tandem, they carried the boxes inside, depositing each in the room it belonged. With playful banter and laughter, the air reverberated with everyone's chatter. An hour later, the truck was unloaded, and the movers departed.

"I wasn't aware we'd crammed so much into that little

apartment," *Daed* said as he set a box on the kitchen cabi-net. "I thought we'd sorted through most of it before we left Oklahoma."

Ethan opened a box filled with miscellaneous plastic con-tainers with lids. "Might help if you weren't such a pack rat. You never throw anything away."

"Never know when you might need something."

"Well, you'll be the one to unpack them."

Daed happily dug into the boxes. "It's a big *haus* with plenty of storage. There's room for everything. And I know where everything should go."

A sudden shrill bellow cut through the air.

"*Ach*, Liam, give me back my bag!"

Ethan's heart sank. *Now, what was the problem?*

Leaving the kitchen, he dashed toward the commotion. In the living room, a fast and furious skirmish unfolded in front of his eyes. Charity and Liam were engaged in a fierce tussle over an old leather book tote.

"Give it back!" Charity's voice crackled with a mixture of anger and frustration. "It's mine!"

Liam smirked, delighting in her visible annoyance. With a twinkle in his eye, he playfully swung the bag above his head. "I wonder what you've got inside that's so important?"

She made a jump to grab it. "Stop teasing me!"

"If you want it," Liam taunted, dangling it out of her reach, "try harder."

"Stop," Charity protested, voice trembling with frustra-tion and panic.

Liam was relentless, savoring the opportunity to annoy her. With a chuckle, he dangled the tote from hand to hand, slipping away from Charity's earnest attempts to grab it back. Desperate to reclaim it, she lunged forward, giving him a hard shove. Liam stumbled over a pile of boxes and fell flat.

Seizing her chance, Charity grabbed her bag. But Liam refused to let go, clutching the frayed leather strap. A vicious tug-of-war ensued. The tote's seams gave way, ripping in half. The contents inside scattered.

Lasting less than a minute, the argument was over as quickly as it began.

"Stop it!" Ethan cried, stepping into the middle of the fray. "Both of you."

Charity was the first to point a finger. "Liam took my bag!"

Liam sat up, dusting himself off. "I was just playing around."

"He tore it. Now it's ruined," she moaned.

Ethan shot a frown. "Now, you've got something else to pay for," he said, admonishing his oldest.

Realizing he'd gone too far, Liam's smug expression crumbled. "Guess so."

"No guessing about it. You will."

"This is my stuff." Bursting into tears, Charity dropped to her knees to recover her belongings. A gift from *Poppi*, she kept all her treasures tucked inside. No one was allowed to open it. "He didn't have any right to take it."

Ethan kneeled to help her. "Let's get your things picked up."

A pack of gum, a ChapStick, a brush and hair ties, a bottle of water and a candy bar were things he expected to see. So were the books she'd checked out from the library. But there was more. A packet of letters. Carefully tied with a ribbon, they were lying there exposed for all to see.

"Those are mine!" Charity grabbed at the bundle.

Ethan got them first. Believing them to be notes from relatives and friends in Oklahoma, he sorted through them. There was at least a dozen. Dismay widened his eyes. All were addressed to a stranger, *Lew C.*

Confusion washed over him, clouding his mind. The name was unfamiliar. The address was not. It was his. He'd rented the post office box shortly after moving to Burr Oak. He rarely checked it. One of Charity's daily chores was to collect the mail.

Puzzled, his gaze shifted to the top left corner of the envelopes. Dashed in a feminine hand, a woman's name and address filled the space. *Beth Spangler.* She, too, corresponded through a post office box. Curiosity intertwined with apprehension. Silence hung in the air, heavy with the weight of discovery.

He held out the stack. "Who do these belong to?"

Chapter Thirteen

Thoughts racing, Ethan attempted to sort through the story of the letters as his daughter tried to explain their presence in her book bag. Apprehension painted her face. Hands fidgeting in her lap, she struggled to meet his gaze. The atmosphere felt heavy and somber as the details began to unfold.

"You were trying to find *eine ehefrau* for me?" he asked, incredulously.

Face flushed, Charity lowered her gaze. *"Ja."*

"Whatever gave you the idea to do that?"

"Poppi did," she whispered.

Daed's brows rose. "Me?"

She gave her *groossdaadi* an earnest look. "I heard you talking about the social ads. You said *Datt* should write to one of the *frauleins*."

"Ach, that's true. I did say it might do you *gut t*o make a new lady *freundin.*"

Flabbergasted, Ethan sucked in a breath. "I remember." At the time, he'd declined the idea. He wasn't an eloquent writer and couldn't imagine reaching out to a stranger. He couldn't help but feel inadequate, fearing he'd fail to capture the essence of his feelings on paper. Expressing his emotions was hard enough in person. His strength resided in the honest toil of his hands and the devotion he displayed in every aspect of his life.

Tears welled up in Charity's eyes, threatening to spill over as she summoned the courage to explain. "I wanted *Datt* to have someone..." she said, swiping at damp eyes. "So he wouldn't be sad anymore."

"You answered one of the ads?"

"Ja."

Once again, Ethan sorted through the envelopes. By the look of things, a lively correspondence had taken place. On one hand, he felt touched by his daughter's attempt to fill the void left by her *mamm's* passing. On the other, he felt a growing sense of unease. The letters written on his behalf were done without his knowledge. He hadn't written a single word.

Still, it was hard to be angry. No doubt compassion had motivated Charity's actions, as did the love she held for him. It was also a poignant reminder her heart ached, too. Pricilla's death tore a gaping hole in their lives. His daughter was trying to make their lives whole again. Happy.

"I understand what you were trying to do," he conceded, laying the stack on the table. "But it was wrong. This *fraulein* you've been writing—"

"Beth. Her name is Beth Spangler."

"A *gut* Amish name," *Daed* interjected. "I like it."

"She a nice lady."

"I'm sure she's a sweet woman. But that's beside the point." He tapped the stack. "You may have meant no harm, but you deceived an innocent person."

Voice trembling, Charity summoned the courage to protest. "I didn't mean to."

"I do not doubt your heart was in the right place. But it wasn't the path to take. What you did was wrong."

Charity shifted uncomfortably. The weight of her actions pressed heavily on her shoulders. She looked very young then, vulnerable and lost. "I guess so."

Slumped back in his chair, Liam raised his head. "It was pretty ignorant," he muttered, swiping a hand beneath his nose.

Hackles rose. "You shouldn't have torn my book bag," she asserted.

Ethan shot a stern frown at both. "Please, stop. I've heard enough arguing from both of you."

Liam chuffed. "Can I go?" He glanced toward the living room. "I want to get my stuff unpacked."

"Yes, but you're not off the hook yet. Your stunt is going to cost your cell phone two extra months."

"But!"

"Don't start. I'm not in the mood."

Liam stood up. "Fine. I'll take it." Stomping into the living room, he picked up a box. Disappearing down the hall, he went into his room. "I don't need the stupid thing, anyway," he called back before kicking the door shut with his foot.

"Can I go, too?" Charity asked.

"*Nein.* We still have to figure out this mess." The damage was done. How to deal with the fallout had yet to be decided.

More silence followed.

Then Charity asked, "Am I in trouble?"

"I don't know." Ethan glanced at the incriminating evidence. "It's not that you wrote the letters. It's that you misrepresented who was doing the writing. Beth believes she's corresponding with a real person—not someone you made up."

"I didn't make anything up," she whispered. "I used the letters of our first names to make a name. And I told her all about us."

"How did you fool her into believing you were a grown man?"

"Miss Pressler helped me."

"The librarian?"

"I told her I was writing a story. Miss Pressler showed

me how to use the computer so I could look things up on the internet. How to write letters and stuff like that."

Daed unexpectedly chuckled. "Charity always was the clever one."

A blush reddened her cheeks. "The words weren't all mine," she admitted after a long pause. "I copied some of it."

Ethan swiped a hand across his brow. Had the offense not been so serious, he might have admired her creativity and imagination. An advanced reader, Charity was usually several grade levels ahead of other students.

She fidgeted nervously, floundering as the complications of her fraud deepened. "I'm sorry. I messed up, didn't I?"

"*Ja.* You did," he said. "I hope you are paying attention to the lesson *Gott* gave you today. The Lord warns that deception will be uncovered, and the truth will come to light."

Visibly shaken, she returned an earnest look. "Is *Gott* going to punish me?"

Ethan's senses wavered between the sternness expected of him and the unconditional love he held for his youngest. "*Gott* will forgive you. And so will I. I know you didn't think about it, but your charade could only go so far. What were you going to do if Beth asked to meet in person?"

Charity's hands fidgeted with the frayed edge of her apron. Distress clouded her expression. "I—I don't know. I liked getting her letters. It gave me something to look forward to. She's so nice. It was like having a special *freundin*."

Her words struck a chord. Ethan knew deep down his daughter needed more than a father's love. She needed a woman's tender touch. Desperately. Right then and there, he made a solemn vow. He would let go of the fear of falling in love once more, and trust *Gott* to guide him to the one who would bring warmth and companionship to his *familie* again.

Daed leaned forward. "Now that you know the truth, perhaps you should write and explain. If Beth's got *youngies*, she will probably understand and laugh."

"I just got a letter from her." The flickering lamp illuminated the hope in Charity's anxious gaze. "I haven't answered."

"And you're not going to. This exchange must stop. Immediately."

Dismay widened her eyes. "But Beth will expect me to write back."

"Absolutely not. The lie must stop. Today." His tone left no room for discussion. "Do you understand?"

"Ja." She went limp, slumping over the table. "I won't write another."

Ethan's gaze traveled over her dejected figure. Blessed with curiosity and intelligence, his daughter had accidentally tangled herself in a web of mischief. In her mind, her actions made perfect sense. A single lady needed an *ehmann*. He needed an *ehefrau*. Why wouldn't it work?

"Are you still mad?"

Startled out of his thoughts, Ethan shook his head. *"Nein.* I'm not."

"I won't lie to anyone, ever again," she said, and then finished with a sincere resolution. "I promise."

"You're forgiven." Legs cramped from sitting, Ethan pushed away from the table. "We still have unpacking to do. Go to your room and make up your bed." Embracing her shoulder, he gave her a gentle kiss on the forehead. "We'll deal with the rest of it tomorrow."

Hugging him back, Charity sniffled softly. "Okay." She slipped out of his embrace, and then turned and left the kitchen. The sound of each footfall reverberated in the silence, echoing through the space.

Shadows shifted as the sun dipped closer to the far horizon. The day, so exciting and full of activity, had come to an end.

Daed rose to light an oil lamp. His gnarled hands trembled slightly as he adjusted the flame. The flickering light illuminated the kitchen, casting shadows around the unfamiliar space.

Ethan glanced across the table. The lamplight reflected off the old man's silver beard, deepening the lines etched into his weathered face. "The changes have been hard on all of us, but it's going to get better now that we've settled down in a real home."

Daed nodded. "I pray the Lord is listening."

"You should go to bed. I'll finish up here."

"I have to admit, I'm tuckered out." Energy drained, *Daed* claimed a lamp. *"Gute nacht, mein sohn."* His stooped walk held a hint of weariness as he shuffled toward his bedroom.

Content to sit, Ethan glanced out the wide kitchen window. Where had the time gone? The sky outside presented swirls of fiery orange, vibrant pink, and the softest tinge of lavender. All blended harmoniously as if *Gott* was crafting a masterpiece. The luminous canvas slowly transformed, casting its enchanting picture over the land. A breeze rose, whispering through the sturdy oak trees. Nestled amid the pastoral beauty of the countryside, the *haus* was perfect in every way.

He cocked his head, listening to the sounds throughout. The muffled melody of pop music emanated from Liam's room. Portable and powered by battery, radios provided a way to keep up with news in the community, including storms and other emergency warnings. Though gospel was his preferred choice of music, he occasionally snapped his fingers to the twang of a country tune. Walking on tiptoes, Charity was quiet as a mouse.

Cherishing the moment of peaceful reflection, he released a sigh. Despite the trouble of the day, the new place already felt like home.

His gaze drifted toward the letters he'd confiscated.

Curiosity piqued, he reached for an envelope. Plain and white, the handwriting on its face was flowery and very feminine. Extracting a page, he began to read. Soon, he was caught in an engaging narrative. The eloquent script danced across the pages, overflowing with warmth, empathy and a profound love of the Lord.

Lowering the last page, a sense of longing washed over him. The letters possessed a familiarity that resonated deeply, hinting at a connection he dared not voice aloud. There was something about the tone, a familiar cadence, that struck a chord deep within him. He couldn't quite put his finger on it, but the feeling intensified with each passing line. Through the narrative, several revealing details emerged. Among other things, the woman wrote about her *familie* and farm, the shop she kept and her hobbies. Taken one by one, it could have been any Amish woman living in a rural community. Strung together the details created an evocative image.

Anticipation heightened, he scrubbed a hand across his face. Recognition flickered beneath his composed exterior. *Surely, it's not...*

The interior of the post office box was empty, devoid of any signs of correspondence.

"Nothing today?" Emily asked.

"Nein." Spirit sinking, Amity closed the latch and locked the box. Checking the mail every day had become an addiction. When a letter arrived, she was ecstatic. When nothing came, disappointment flooded her.

Sophie, with her kind eyes and auburn curls tucked beneath her *kapp*, chimed in. "Perhaps the letter has been delayed. Or lost."

"It may yet find its way to your hands," Emily added, her voice brimming with optimism.

Amity pursed her lips. A pang of disappointment gripped her insides. Nearly a month had passed without a reply. She usually received something a few days after sending hers. But her box remained empty. Aside from junk mail, she'd received nothing. It was painfully obvious their correspondence had ended. The snub delivered a bitter sting.

"I think I've been dumped."

"Surely not," Emily scoffed. "Lew seemed like such a steadfast fellow."

"It could be he's gotten busy, with work," Sophie added. A touch of worry etched her brow. "Perhaps an unexpected illness."

"I suppose that's possible." Nevertheless, the weight of uncertainty pressed on her shoulders. Doubt crept in, casting a shadow over the sincerity of their correspondence. Believing her mystery man to be sincere, she'd shared her hopes and dreams. Each word he'd written back was woven into the fabric of her emotions. She'd cherished the bond they'd forged, exchanging tales of their lives and plans for the future. And then he'd coldly severed the thread. The abruptness of his silence caught her off guard, leaving her adrift.

Was he playing a cruel trick, a prankster masquerading behind eloquent words? An intricate scenario of deception and betrayal wove its way through her thoughts. Emotions adrift, her mind spun with questions.

Emily gave her a reassuring pat. "He'll write. I'm sure of it."

"Don't give up so soon," Sophie echoed.

"I don't care if he ever does," she declared, feeling quite out of sorts. *No more ads, no more pen pals*. "I've no time for this nonsense. I have a shop to open and a living to make."

Leaving the post office behind, the three set off toward their destination. The gentle clip-clop of horse hooves clattered on the cobblestones as wagons skillfully avoided gas-powered vehicles.

"Wasn't Lettie Stohl supposed to drop off some of her gourd birdhouses the morning?" Emily asked.

Amity nodded. "They're quite clever. And she paints them so beautifully."

"I'll be packing and sending them out this afternoon," Sophie added. "We've had orders for half a dozen since they went up on the website."

The conversation prompted Amity to remember her dilemma wasn't dire. Others were facing much harder trials. Recently a young widow had come into the shop, asking to sell her crafts on consignment. Attempting to support a newborn and her other young *kinder*, Lettie made birdhouses out of large gourds, painting each with unique floral designs. The samples she provided sold within hours to *Englisch* shoppers. Delighted to be earning some money, Lettie promised to bring in more of her crafts.

Knowing others were facing hard times, Amity kept her commission low. Offering a platform that allowed others to sell their wares was her way of giving back to the community. Busy keeping home and hearth together, many crafty Amish women were grateful to leave the selling to someone else. In tough times, it gave them a way to contribute to the *familie* budget. In some cases, such as Lettie's, it meant the ability to keep food on the table and dignity intact.

As expected, the *kaffeeshop* was open by the time they arrived. Arriving at the crack of dawn to take delivery of foodstuffs and other supplies, Ethan would unlock the shared front entrance and turn on the lights. The inviting scent of baked goods and freshly ground *kaffee* wafted through the air, filling the building with delicious aromas. The shared foyer brimmed with customers enjoying their morning beverage and breakfast before heading off to their busy day.

Amity unlocked the door to her shop, then entered and bustled about. Every item was lovingly organized with meticulous attention to detail. Her memory journeyed back to the day she decided to establish her business. It was not an easy decision for an Amish woman. The allure of the *Englisch* world often whispered tempting promises of convenience and wealth. Yet, she'd felt a stirring within her, a conviction this was the path laid before her by the Lord. She felt the presence of *Gott* guiding her, infusing her once again to remain true to the traditions of a simpler life.

"We've forgotten our morning prayer," Sophie reminded her. Vivacious and devout, she never failed to lead the daily devotional.

The women all came together, joining hands and lowering their heads. It was a moment each valued and cherished, a chance to refocus and renew their faith.

"Dear Lord," Sophie began in her clear, pure voice. "I ask that you bless my friend Amity, whose heart and desires are pure. She is ready to let in love and I pray she finds a helpmeet who is perfect for her…"

Closing her eyes, Amity listened to the humble words filling her ears. Knowing how disappointed she was, it was kind of her friend to petition for her.

Bless us all, oh, Lord, so we may do gut this day, she silently added. Prayer complete, she opened her eyes. "*Danke* for the lovely prayer," she murmured. A sense of serenity filled her, radiating from within.

Sophie returned a shy smile. "I know you feel let down," she said, demurring under the praise, "but I have a feeling something wonderful is going to happen for you. Soon."

Spirit lighter, Amity nodded.

"I've learned my lesson," she declared. "I'll be content with what *Gott* intends for me to have, not what I think I want." Embracing the day with renewed vigor, she released her disappointment.

Ready to greet customers, the women set about their day. Sophie turned the sign on the door to Open. Emily checked the register, making sure there was plenty of change.

Satisfied everything was in hand, Amity headed into the back office. Part of being a business owner meant payroll and other paperwork needed her attention. To do her paperwork, she relied on a "plain computer" for business purposes. Made to meet the needs of the Amish community, the simple machine offered no gimmicks and didn't connect to the internet. The programs were limited to spreadsheets and word processing. It did have the ability to save files to flash drives and could be connected to a printer.

Humming a favorite tune, she immersed herself in the task. Running the numbers revealed the shop was on track to make a tidy profit. Branching out, into online sales, had more than tripled their revenue. The amount she always set aside each month for community charities had also grown exponentially. Immersed in her calculations, her nimble fingers moved over the keyboard.

As the clock ticked toward noon, a knock on the office door announced the arrival of an unexpected visitor.

Ethan stood in the doorway. *"Störe ich?"* he greeted in *Deitsch. Am I disturbing you?*

Amity looked up. After the disastrous frolic, they rarely spoke. He kept to his side of the building. She kept to hers. An exchange of pleasantries was as far as their conversations went.

She gestured for him to enter. *"Nein.* I was just finishing up."

He stepped inside. "I won't be long," he said and extended an envelope. "My half of the utilities."

She accepted it. *"Danke."* She reached for her receipt book and dashed off a few lines. After tearing out the page, she handed it over. Many Amish still used an old-fashioned ledger for accounting.

Ethan carefully folded the receipt and tucked it in his pocket. "I appreciate it."

Unspoken tension lingered in the air, burdening the space between them.

As they had to share the building and its upkeep, there was no reason not to be amiable. "You are well since the move?" Relocating his *familie* to the Klatch farm had put distance between them. She never saw Wayne, Liam or Charity anymore. New faces staffed the *kaffeeshop*.

"Ja. Daed loves the country and doesn't come to town unless he has to. *Youngies* are doing well, too. Charity has a job at the library. She's a helper, shelving books in the afternoons. She does story time, too. Reading to the littles."

"Sounds perfect."

"It is. Liam's doing *gut*, too. He likes his job at the ranch. He plans to enter the junior rodeo next March when the season starts again. It'll give him all winter to practice."

"Glad to hear it all worked out. You look happy, too."

"I am." Hesitation flickering, Ethan cleared his throat. "Still writing that fella?"

Regret pressed hard. *"Nein,"* she said, feigning indifference. "He's moved on. And so have I." The weight of her confession settled on her shoulders like a yoke, burdening her with the consequences of her choices.

"Sorry to hear it."

"It didn't work out." Despite her nonchalance, sorrow, confusion and self-doubt clenched hard. No one wanted to admit they'd been dumped.

Compassion filled his eyes. "I know you hoped it would."

Something in his tone thrummed Amity's senses. Now that the blur of infatuation had dissipated, she couldn't fail to glimpse Ethan in an entirely new light. In his sturdy figure, she realized what might have been.

I was a fool to say no.

Instead of paying attention to the man who'd offered a secure future, she'd tossed him aside, turning down a legitimate proposal in favor of a wraith who existed only on paper. Why? Because she dreamed of romance. And Ethan, with his gruff, inelegant manner, didn't seem to have a tender bone in his body. Entranced by the notion of hearts and flowers, she'd allowed a mystery correspondent to turn her head away from the things that mattered. A man who worked hard, who valued faith and *familie*, was a far more valuable treasure than one who hid behind flattering words.

Unable to form a reply, she pursed her lips. She had nothing else to offer to the conversation.

Ethan offered a tentative smile. "If you need to talk, I always have a cup of *kaffee* ready."

"*Danke*. That's kind of you. I might do that." Her answer rang hollow.

He jerked a thumb. "I need to get back. To work."

"Me, too." She longed to say more, but a knot formed in her throat.

Ethan departed. He did not glance back.

Watching him go, a profound sense of loss enveloped her. Her heart pounded a rhythm that mirrored her deep sorrow.

Tears welled up. How she longed to call his name, to beckon him back and undo the cruel act that had fractured their friendship. But her chance to share his life had passed, seeping away like sand through an hourglass.

Chapter Fourteen

The hour was late. And he was alone.

Slipping his hand into a drawer, Ethan retrieved the letters he'd tucked away. While he'd considered destroying proof of Charity's deception, a small inner voice had compelled him to hold on to them.

Taking a seat by the hearth, he pulled a few pages out on an envelope. His heart skipped a beat as he read through the pages again. The script filling the pages was familiar. The swirly feminine penmanship was the same as that on the receipt Amity had given him earlier that day. She'd also confirmed her pen pal's correspondence had ended.

Coincidence?

Ethan's pulse sped up. He was certain it wasn't. In his mind, the mystery woman's identity was crystal clear.

A torrent of emotions washed over him. Memories flooded his mind—the times they had stolen glances at each other during community gatherings, the secret smiles that spoke volumes when they couldn't find the words. He felt a deep connection to her, one that transcended the masks they'd always concealed their true feelings behind. It was easy to imagine the possibilities, to envision a life where they walked hand in hand, happy to bask in each other's company.

"I thought I heard a noise." Dressed in his robe and slippers, *Daed* padded into the living room. The warm glow of flames cast flickering shadows around his sturdy figure. "What have you got there?" He claimed the opposite chair. Unpacked and put in their place, cherished possessions filled what had been an impersonal space, turning the empty *haus* into a nurturing sanctuary.

Ethan attempted to tuck the pages away, but a few fluttered from his grasp. "Nothing," he mumbled, lunging to reclaim them. His fingers, normally nimble, felt clumsy.

Daed's sharp gaze followed his move. "You kept them?"

He retrieved the pages. *"Ja."* He'd read them, too. Many times over. Through the strokes of her pen, she poured out her thoughts, as if whispering directly into his ear.

A knowing smile graced the old man's weathered lips as he took the opposite chair. "I would have, too." He chuckled. "And then I'd be curious. Who could she be?"

Believing the veil of secrecy to be lifted, Ethan's pulse raced. "I believe I know," he admitted, tucking the pages away.

"Do you?"

Ethan nodded. "It's Amity."

Daed's mouth dropped open. "Are you sure?"

Explaining his suspicions, Ethan filled in the details. "Everything fits."

"Ha!" *Daed* said, slapping his knee with unexpected glee. "I knew it."

"Knew what?"

"That you and Amity were meant for each other."

Embarrassment tightened Ethan's throat. "I asked her to be my *ehefrau*," he reminded his father. *"Sie sagte nein,"* he said, slipping into *Deitsch*.

Daed returned a narrow look. "I don't blame her. I'd have said the same if you'd have come around asking like it was a job interview." He reached out and swatted at Ethan as one would a nippy puppy. "What were you thinking?"

"That I needed an *ehefrau*."

"Aye, you do." *Daed* guffawed, rolling his eyes. "But it's a lifetime commitment. And a *fraulein* expects more than the asking. One of the things you've got to do is take her on a walkabout. Don't know what courting is nowadays, but I'd say women still expect a fella to show courtesy and appreciation."

Chastened, Ethan dropped his gaze. He knew all that. And he'd done everything wrong. "I think I love her." Even as he spoke, a bittersweet ache consumed his heart.

"Don't think it. Know it. If it's true and meant to be, tell her how you feel."

"I've let her down in so many ways." He gave the packet of letters a shake. "And then there's this deception. She'd never forgive me if she knew the truth."

"Are you so sure? Seems to me, she's the forgiving sort." *Daed* cocked his head. "Maybe you've forgotten how you treated her when you first met."

Ethan winced. "I wasn't kind."

"You were a silly old mule," *Daed* reminded him. "Kicking fits when something didn't go your way. But Amity—she never said a cross word back. And she extended a hand to help both your *youngies*. Why, any man who lets a woman like that get away is a *täuschen*. A fool. And if you want me to say it twice, I will."

Ethan spread his hands helplessly. "I don't know what to do."

"I believe *Gott* has given you a chance to make things right." *Daed's* gaze settled on the letters. "The answer is in your own hands."

"Are you saying I should write her back?" Uncertainty tinged his question.

"Charity said the last letter hadn't been answered. She's expecting one. This time, *you* do the writing. Ask to meet, face-to-face. Then you can try and make things right with her."

Ethan's shoulders drooped. "If only it was that easy."

Releasing a sigh, *Daed* pushed himself out of his chair. Pausing, he placed a hand on Ethan's shoulder. His solid touch carried decades of experience. "Pray on the matter and let *Gott* lead. Charity might have started this, but it's up to you to finish it." Answer given, he nodded toward the kitchen. "Think I could use a cup of hot milk to help me sleep." Hand falling away, he shuffled toward his destination.

Silence once again filled the room.

Ethan glanced at the letters. Would it be that easy to make amends?

Doubt crept in like shadows on a moonlit night. How did Amity feel about him? What if the attraction was strictly one-sided? Stepping up and assuming the identity of her pen pal might backfire most spectacularly.

What if she doesn't see beyond our differences?

The urge to fling the letters into the fire caused his hand to tremble. Resisting the impulse, he tucked them out of sight and closed the drawer.

Unsettled and uncertain, he glanced around the shadowy room. *Daed* puttered in the kitchen, making himself something to drink. Liam and Charity were asleep.

He rose from his place, went into his room and shut the door. After lighting a lamp, he claimed his Bible from its place beside his bed. Taking a seat at his desk, he began to read. As if led to the answer, his gaze fell to Proverbs 31:10: *Who can find a virtuous woman... She will do him good and not evil... And worketh willingly with her hands.*

The weight of the newfound realization settled upon his shoulders. That was Amity. Virtuous and kind, she toiled without complaint.

The chance to start over was there. He just needed to find the courage to follow through.

It didn't matter who had started the correspondence or why. He would take the responsibility…and bear the repercussions. It was the right thing to do. It was the only thing to do.

Under the soft glow of lamplight, Ethan took out a few sheets of paper. Writing carefully, he attempted to craft the words that mirrored the depths of his emotions.

Dearest, he jotted, his voice trembling as he read back the inked lines. *I humbly beseech you to grant me a moment of your time, for I find myself unable to silence the whispers of my conscience any longer…* More words came in a rush, pouring out across the page. *I have prayed deeply on the matter, and it is with unwavering conviction I believe the Lord has led me to…*

As each stroke of his pen dashed across the page, he poured his heart out on the paper, hoping his words would convey the depth of his affection. He yearned to share his life with the woman who had illuminated his world in so many ways, even if it meant venturing into uncharted territories. The pain haunting his past was no longer at the forefront of his mind. Building a new life, learning to live again—and to love again—was.

Before he could change his mind, Ethan sealed the letter and addressed it. He'd mail it when he got to town in the morning. Given the travel of the local post, it would take no more than a day or two to reach her. He'd asked to meet, naming a time and place.

One of two things would happen. She would show up. Or

she would send a reply declining. He refused to consider the third option: that she would entirely ignore it.

Anticipation gripped hard. He knew not what the future held. But he was prepared to take a leap of faith, armed with the belief that *Gott* had shown him the path to make things right with the woman who'd captured his heart. The emotions he'd kept hidden for so long were now set free, soaring with the promise of possibility. He would embrace life's uncertainties with faith and courage, trusting that the path he walked, no matter how winding, would lead him where he needed to be.

Closing his eyes, he bowed his head and sent an earnest entreaty to the heavens.

Oh, merciful Father, guide this letter to the one I love. Soften her heart and grant her the grace to give me a second chance.

As he finished his prayer, a sense of peace settled within him, as if his words had reached divine ears and were received with understanding. His spirit renewed, the flickering oil lamp on the table seemed to burn brighter, casting its gentle glow across the room. With each passing second, he became more certain he'd made the right choice.

But would Amity choose him?

Today was the day.

Gathering her resolve, Amity dressed in her best frock before carefully donning her prayer *kapp* and apron. As she went through the motions of dressing, she glanced at her reflection in the mirror. Her gaze bore traces of anxiety and wistfulness. Come noon, she'd finally meet her mystery correspondent.

Tucking his letter into her handbasket, she hurried to lock her door and head toward church. The journey on foot wasn't far. The quaint white building soon came into view. Clad in simple yet elegant attire, familiar faces greeted her with wide smiles and gentle nods. She joined her *schwesters* and they sat together, sharing warm glances during hymns, and finding comfort in each other's presence. Only Florene was missing. Her absence was a painful reminder of the strife that had torn their *familie* asunder.

Seated amid those she loved, Amity tried to immerse herself in the bishop's sermon. Though the fellowship was a balm to her soul, it also reminded her she was still very much alone in this world. After the long service concluded, the other churchgoers gathered in circles, chatting and laughing merrily. She tried to join the conversations but found it impossible to concentrate on anything but the meeting ahead.

Pulse thudding with nervousness, Amity closed her eyes. Reading the pages a dozen times over, she'd memorized every word.

Meet me at the gazebo after Sunday service on the 19th, he'd written. *I'll explain everything.* Oddly, his handwriting had changed. The neat script seemed more forceful, and mature, as if he were ready to reveal his true self.

The wait—five long days—had been excruciating. Through the long hours of preaching, she'd searched the pews, wondering whom he might be.

Gathering her nerve, she broke away from the group. The prospect of meeting her pen pal was thrilling and nerve-wracking. She wondered if the man she had poured her heart out to through ink and paper would be everything she had imagined.

A haven of tranquility, the structure tucked into the church garden was a recent addition. Vibrant roses surrounded its perimeter. Delicate lavender bushes painted a colorful tapestry along the cobblestone path leading to the wooden steps.

A gentle breeze ruffled the air, carrying the melodic serenade of birdsong. Installed by church elders, the quaint pavilion had a special role in the community's customs, a place where courtship unfurled its tender wings. Following Sunday services, men and women often sat together. In plain view, it was a charming way to publicly declare their intentions to each other.

No one was there.

Nervous and fretful, Amity considered leaving. But, no. It would mean going back to square one. Once again, she would have nobody. The correspondence had given her hope. That somewhere out there was someone meant to share her life.

Gathering her courage, she took a seat on a bench. Hands clasped, she looked out over the garden. Several long minutes passed. One fellow walked by. And then another. Both offered pleasant smiles but showed no interest. She wondered what he looked like. Her imagination painted vivid images, but none seemed to come together.

The minutes kept ticking away.

No one came.

Doubt crept in. What if he had changed his mind? Had she been played for a fool?

She wouldn't have to wait much longer to find out.

A tall, sturdy figure emerged onto the pathway, walking with a purposeful stride. Dressed in his best, the fellow was indeed as he'd described himself. Clean-shaven, his straw hat was pulled low over his eyes, concealing half his features. Reaching the steps, he lifted his head, offering a clear view of his face.

Recognition struck like a bolt of lightning. Surely, it wasn't *him*?

The irony was almost too much to bear. The air crackled with tension, uncertainty, and unspoken emotions.

Her visitor found his voice first, breaking the silence as he asked hesitantly, "Not who you were expecting?"

She stared, unable to blink. "I didn't think it would be—"

"Me?" he said, finishing for her.

Amity struggled to find the words, but they wouldn't come. It shocked her how different Ethan Zehr looked. Shaving off his heavy beard had completely transformed his face. His sharp jawline and well-defined features were unveiled like a masterpiece long hidden behind cobwebs. The years seemed to rewind, giving him a youthful look. The stress lines that had etched their way around his eyes seemed to have retreated, and his gaze sparkled with newfound light. The simple act had bestowed a remarkable change. He looked like an entirely different man.

Taking another step up, he offered a bashful smile. His eyes betrayed a hint of nerves. "I hope you're not disappointed." As if to prove he had a right to be there, he produced a familiar envelope. "It's nice to meet you, Miss Spangler."

Amity glanced at the letter. There was no mistaking it. The handwriting across its face was her own. It was the last one she'd written before the silence set in.

Curiosity prodded her. Why the delay in answering? And why now, after such a long silence?

Thoughts reeling with unanswered questions, she retrieved his from her basket. "Likewise, Mr. Lew C."

They looked at each other awkwardly. It occurred to her that they were right back where they'd started. Which wasn't anywhere at all. The pen pal carefully masked under a veil of anonymity now stared back at her. The man she had turned away was the very one who had stolen her heart through ink and parchment. The same man whose proposal she'd been too prideful to accept.

Warmth embraced her cheeks, painting them with a rosy hue. Frustration knotted her stomach. What a fine mess she'd created. Had there been a hole to crawl into, she would have gladly borrowed it to bury herself.

Oh, what a tangled web I've woven, she silently lamented. The moment she'd dreamt of, she now dreaded.

Irony teased his fine mouth. "You don't look pleased."

Amity stared at him crossly. As far as she was concerned, nothing was amusing about the entire situation. Had he forgotten so quickly how cruelly she'd treated him?

Guilt immediately settled on her shoulders. Regret gnawed at her conscience. She'd rebuffed him, disregarding his feelings. He had her backed into a corner, and he knew it. Like a cat stalking a mouse, he'd found the perfect moment to pounce. He had every right to chew her up and spit her out. She wouldn't blame him if he did.

"Now that you know it's me, you can't want to stay," she said, flinging out the words and attempting to push him away verbally.

Ethan stepped closer, removing his hat. A fall of dark curls drifted around his handsome face. "Oh, but I do," he said, and then explained, "When I read the letters, I prayed you were the woman who sent them. And when I answered, I prayed you were the one they would go to." No anger tinged his voice. Quite the opposite. He sounded completely sincere.

Amity stared, dumbfounded. This time around, she was the one who'd come with expectations in hand. He had every right to reject her. "But I—I said *nein* to your proposal," she stammered. "Why would you want to see me again?"

He visibly drew a breath. "Because I want another chance."

Astonishment plucked the air out of her lungs. Had she heard correctly? "You do?"

"*Ja.*"

One simple word was all he said. *Yes.*

The world seemed to hold its breath in the silence that followed. Butterflies that had once fluttered with excitement now seemed to be suspended in midair as if waiting for a resolution to his momentous confession. The air around them was charged with a mix of anticipation and trepidation. The fierce and unyielding affection that had always simmered between them was palpable. And undeniable.

I do love him.

Nervous excitement accompanied her newfound awareness. Was there a way to turn things around? Myriad emotions surged through her, like the wild winds that swept through the fields during a thunderstorm. She struggled to retain her composure. "What happens next?"

Ethan claimed the bench across from hers. "We start over," he said, setting his hat to one side.

A delightful tingling sensation danced down her spine, leaving her feeling both lightheaded and grounded, as if she was floating and rooted simultaneously. Amid the chaos twisting her mind into knots, hope stirred the embers of emotion.

"Are you sure? I mean, we're both Amish...but still so different."

He laughed. *"Anders ist gut,"* he answered in *Deitsch.* "I'll learn to adapt. Just like *Daed* did."

Fear and uncertainty mingled with hope and anticipation. Could they navigate the challenges that lay ahead?

"I—I can't change. I'll always speak my mind."

"And I'll always listen because you're usually right." His voice caressed her senses like a gentle melody. "You brought me back to life inside. I know it's all right to go on, to be happy again." His gaze intensified, penetrating hers with seriousness. "I want you to be a part of that happiness."

"You mean that?" Her voice was barely a squeak.

He nodded. "I messed up the first time. I know that. But I want to make things right. To court you properly." Nervous determination fueled his words. "I know it won't be easy. And it won't happen overnight. But I'm willing to try." Seeming to realize the depth of her uncertainty, he leaned forward and extended his hands toward her. "Please—give me a chance to prove I'm a man worth having."

Amity glanced at his hands, and then at her own. His were large and roughened from hard work. Her were small and delicate, but no less chapped from daily toil. She couldn't be sure, but it looked like her hands would fit into his just fine. Still, caution whispered in her ear, reminding her of the disappointment she had endured before. Conflicting emotions wrestled, each determined to have its say. Whispers of a chance unexplored echoed through her mind like the distant call of a faraway song.

Hesitation held her back. She'd been burned before. Badly. Desire was more than just words. It meant action. And sacrifices.

"You're sure I'm who you want?"

Ethan visibly drew a deep breath. "I am. I always knew you were the one. I was just too stubborn to admit it."

Amity gazed into his eyes. There, she saw the unyielding resolve of a man unwilling to give up. She also saw a reflection of the life she could lead. One filled with love and happiness.

At that moment, something extraordinary happened. She believed him.

The boundaries separating them dissolved. The authenticity of their feelings stood firm. This wasn't a cruel twist of fate; it was a second chance, an opportunity to rewrite their story, to mend the wounds that had kept them apart.

With courage as her compass and trust as her guide, Amity slipped her hands into his. Skin brushed skin as his strong fingers closed around hers. His touch was an electric spark, igniting the enchanting dance of emotions they both felt, but had never dared to voice. Hands clasped, their souls intertwined. The past crumbled away, leaving behind only the raw essence of acceptance.

Without uttering a word, they both understood the significance of their commitment. An Amish man and woman not only connected for themselves, but also for the community and the church. And for the future *kinder* they hoped to have. Forgiveness and second chances were woven into the fabric of their faith.

It was a leap she was ready to take.

Neither noticed when members of the *Leit* strolled by. The church elders looked on with approving nods, pleased to see another young couple declare their feelings for all to see.

Bishop Harrison smiled with satisfaction, pleased he'd been proven right. "You've got the bird in hand."

One of the deacons walking with him grinned. "Don't let her go now," he teased in the way men always did.

"Never," Ethan called back. "She's going to be mine, and I want everyone to know it." His gaze met hers. "At least, I hope you will be."

Amity's emotions surged, washing away the barriers she'd built around her heart. All the years of waiting, the self-doubt and the whispers of others melted away. *"Ja,"* she murmured. "I am."

Ethan's lips curved into a tender smile. "You can't know how happy I am to hear you say that." Gently tracing the outline of her cheek, he leaned closer, bridging the divide between them. His lips brushed hers, the beginning of a soft, tender kiss. Time seemed to stand still as they surrendered to the beauty of the moment.

Pulling away to catch her breath, Amity sent up a silent prayer of thanks to *Gott*. A gentle breeze swept through the afternoon, stirring a sense of tranquility. The nearby church was a serene witness to the happy occasion.

Everything faded into a distant blur, as if only the two of them existed, cocooned in an intimate world of their own. In that small corner of the garden, two souls found each other, knowing that love, in all its complexity, was the greatest gift they could ever receive. Hand in hand, they prepared to forge a new path, ready to pen a new chapter in their intertwined lives.

Together they would face tomorrow, building their future on a foundation of honesty, faith and the blessings of heaven above…

Epilogue

"Are you sure you're ready to give it up?" Joella Beiler asked.

"*Ja*. It's time." Amity subtly laid a hand on her protruding belly. "I intended to be a stay-at-home *mamm* for a while."

"I think that's wonderful. You must be so excited."

Amity grinned. "Deliriously."

Joella smiled back. "*Danke* for all you've done."

Dipping a hand into her apron pocket, Amity's fingers curled around a set of keys. Plucking them out, she handed them over. "I know you'll do fine."

"I'm grateful to have a place for Colin to grow up." Turning her head, Joella glanced toward the young *boi* playing quietly near the counter. Leaving the remote community of Beeville, she'd come seeking a fresh start after the death of her *ehmann*. Accepting a position as assistant store manager, she'd proved to be a reliable worker.

"I'm happy it worked out. You earned the promotion."

"I'll take *gut* care of your shop."

"I'm not leaving permanently," she said. "Just taking a break."

A few customers stepped into the store, interrupting the conversation.

"*Ach*, excuse me." Joella hurried to greet the newcomers. Engaging the women in conversation, she laughed and chatted merrily. Within minutes, she'd sold several items and was ringing them up at the cash register.

Pleased she'd made the right choice, Amity looked around. *So much has changed.* After she'd accepted Ethan's second proposal to try again, time had flown by in the blink of an eye. That day, now two years gone, they had embarked on a new journey together.

The memories brought a smile. Ethan's patient courtship had warmed her heart, and his genuine love for her filled her with a sense of security. Every slight gesture, every soft touch and every heartfelt conversation deepened their bond.

More images swirled through her mind, vibrant and alive. Their wedding was the most joyous occasion of her life. Their community gathered to celebrate the union, the rustic barn adorned with wildflowers, and the delicious scent of home-cooked meals filling the air. Her heart had fluttered with excitement and nerves as they'd joined hands and spoken their vows, knowing she was about to spend a lifetime with the man who held her heart. True, it hadn't been easy. Their marriage was a journey of growth, forgiveness and understanding. With each step back, they'd taken two forward, becoming stronger as a couple. They'd also discovered *familie* was the most wonderful treasure of all. There was no *his side* or *her side*. It was *theirs*.

Everything had worked out wonderfully. The trials and tribulations they'd faced were a distant memory.

Now a strapping young man of seventeen, Liam had wholeheartedly embraced the cowboy lifestyle. Working with cattle had given him focus and purpose. Enjoying life on the open range, he'd decided not to become a shopkeeper. He belonged on a horse and that was where he intended to stay.

Blossoming into a lovely young *fraulein*, Charity had left school. Working part-time at the library helped her earn spending money. It also gave her access to the computers she needed for her online correspondence courses. Determined to continue her education, she intended to follow her dream to write.

Amity smiled as her stepdaughter's face flashed across her mind's screen. They'd grown close and she treasured their special bond. Given time, the whole truth had revealed itself. Charity confessed to beginning the correspondence that brought them all together.

The letters were tucked away in a wooden chest. Now and again, she would take them out and read them. The Lord—and one mischievous girl—had brought her the love of her life.

Wayne continued to focus on getting his custom *kaffee* blends into the hands of eager consumers. Once online, his business had taken off. Demand was high and he consistently sold out his most popular blends. The income allowed him to build a *dawdy haus* for himself. Puttering around the property, he was quite content.

Growth at the *kaffeshop* next door had forced a drastic change to the building. One whole inner wall had been demolished, taking out the foyer and doubling the seating space for customers. Newly redecorated and expanded, customers came in a steady stream from open to close. Amity's Amish Amenities nestled inside the sheltering walls of the Fellowship Kaffeehaus. Just the way she nestled in her *ehmann's* loving arms after a long day had ended.

The Schroder side was doing well, too. Gail and Levi had welcomed a new *sohn*. Unable to overcome her infertility, Rebecca and Caleb had taken in two foster children. And they were in the process of adopting the pair of orphaned *Englisch* siblings.

The sole ripple of trouble in tranquil waters lay with Florene. Leaving the ranch, she'd cut all contact. No one knew where she was or where she had gone. They could only pray she was alive—somewhere, safe and sound.

Resuming her walk, Amity peeked inside the back offices. Noah was hard at work on his computer, tapping out some mysterious code only he understood. Processing the orders that came in online, Emily and Sophie were busy packing the items for shipping.

"Everything okay?" she asked.

The trio glanced up.

Noah grinned. "We've got it under control, boss."

"You go," Sophie urged. "We'll take care of things here." Weighing a box on the scale, she added the postage.

"You're not even supposed to be on your feet," Emily reminded her.

"I know." The decision to stop working full-time wasn't made lightly. Finely boned and petite, she'd had some trouble carrying and had required a doctor's care. The reason soon became apparent as the months passed. She wasn't carrying one *kind*. She was carrying two. Under her brother-in-law's watchful eye, her pregnancy progressed without complication. The twins were due in a couple of weeks, and everyone was excited beyond measure.

"We can always call if there's an issue," Noah added.

Indeed, they could. Living so far out in the country, where anything could go wrong, Ethan had insisted on getting a cell phone. It wasn't anything fancy, just a simple flip phone. She didn't use it often, but it was handy to have.

The bell above the door tinkled again.

Amity stepped to the front of the store just as Ethan walked inside.

"I wondered where you'd gone," he said as a greeting. The

workday over, he'd removed his denim apron. A vibrant blue spark filled his eyes.

Smiling, Amity silently thanked *Gott* for the blessings bestowed, for the gift of a man who cherished and respected her. She doubted she'd ever over the fact this handsome man belonged to her.

"I was just giving the store keys to Joella and tying up a few loose ends."

He walked up to join her. Beard thicker and longer than ever, he wore it with pride. "You should be resting."

As if to answer for her, a small foot punted her kidney. "Not going to happen soon," she said, cradling her stomach.

Slipping a hand around her waist, Ethan laid his other hand protectively on her belly.

"Going to be a feisty little fella, isn't he?"

She angled her head to look up at him. "Might be a girl doing the kicking."

His grin winded. "Both, I hope."

Amity pulled in a breath as the dynamic duo shifted again. "Me, too." She frowned down on her thick middle. Heavy and uncomfortable, she was ready to deliver the active pair.

Ethan brushed a kiss across her brow. "I can't wait to meet them," he said, giving her a gentle hug. "The anticipation has been one of the best times of my life."

"Mine, too," she said and gazed into his handsome face.

"Time to get you home," he said, and drew her gently toward the door.

Leaning into his strong embrace, Amity allowed him to lead the way. A contented smile lifted her lips as they walked together. Just beyond the threshold lay the path she was born to follow. That of a wife. Mother. Helpmeet to the man she adored. She realized then life was like a patchwork quilt. A tapestry of choices and experiences had woven them together. And they would stay together. For the rest of their lives.

A deep sense of contentment filled her. She was exactly where she was meant to be. Basking in the moment, her emotions began to overflow, filling her with a profound adoration for her husband and the new lives they'd created. As they continued their journey toward tomorrow, she knew their love would endure, a timeless melody that would echo through generations to come.

Just as *Gott* intended.

* * * * *

Dear Reader,

Welcome back to Burr Oak, Texas. I'm so happy you came to visit my little Amish community set in the Lone Star state. I love writing about the Schroder sisters, and it's Amity's turn to find her happily-ever-after. Though she is tiny in stature, Amity's got a great big heart...she also doesn't hesitate to stand up for herself and say exactly what's on her mind. That sometimes creates misunderstandings, but she's always willing to forgive and move on. I wanted to pair her with a man whose faith and determination were as strong as her own. Widower Ethan Zehr also has a stubborn streak. And when two strong personalities collide, sparks are bound to fly!

If this is your first visit to Burr Oak, I hope you will check out other books in the Texas Amish Brides series. Stop by and visit me online at www.pameladesmondwright.com. You can browse all my Love Inspired releases...and find out what's coming next. While you're there, don't forget to sign up for updates, sent straight to your inbox!

I love hearing from readers, and you can contact me by snail mail, too, at PO Box 165, Texico, NM, 88135-0165.

Sending a warm hug to all!
Pamela Desmond Wright

HARLEQUIN
Reader Service

Enjoyed your book?

Try the perfect subscription for Romance readers and get more great books like this delivered right to your door.

See why over 10+ million readers have tried Harlequin Reader Service.

Start with a Free Welcome Collection with free books and a gift—valued over $20.

Choose any series in print or ebook. See website for details and order today:

TryReaderService.com/subscriptions